J.W. Gent.'s The Valiant Scot: A Retelling

David Bruce

Published by David Bruce, 2022.

J.W. GENT.'S THE VALIANT SCOT: A RETELLING

First edition. September 2, 2022.

Copyright © 2022 David Bruce.

ISBN: 979-8215354100

Written by David Bruce.

Table of Contents

Dedication

Dedicated to My Sister Brenda

Brenda wrote, "During COVID and when visitors were restricted from visiting their loved one in the assisted-living facility I worked at, a patient mentioned to me how much she liked spaghetti during a late-night conversation we had. She was a night owl like me. Her name was Dee. I called her "Gerdy." Then she would say, "Dirty Gerdy," and we'd laugh. Anyway, on my way to work I bought two spaghetti meals from Olive Garden. I left for work early that night. I went to work, set up outlet dinners in the dining room, went to her room and wheeled her down to the dining room where we had dinner together. At that time, the residents weren't leaving their room and had their meals alone in their room. It was nighttime and everyone was already in bed, so I didn't see a problem. She was so grateful and had enough food for three more meals. It was such a simple gesture, but during that time it meant so much to her and for me."

Brenda once bought a newspaper at a gas station on Thanksgiving and tipped the female employee $5, and the employee cried.

Brenda wrote, "I do remember that. I also remember when George tipped a TeeJays waitress $100, and she cried. Our family does a lot of good deeds all the time: I unload people's grocery carts when the people are in those electric scooters. If they are alone with a few groceries, I'll leave cash for the cashier to pay for the groceries. I've had a lot of good deeds done to me when I didn't have a lot of money. It feels good to pay it forward."

She added, "I just have one more thing to add and then I'm done. I've had a lot of people in my life do good deeds for me when I was at a low point on my life. I was at a low point for a very long time. David, you know what you've done for me, and I can never thank you enough. Martha paid for antibiotics for me when I had strep throat and didn't have money. Rosa bought me groceries. Carla has done so much, and she had us over for Easter just after Chad died. When I say US, I mean all of my kids. She was so sick and ended up at the Emergency Room that same night. Frank gave me a car. And George buys my gas for me whenever he's in Florida. And Mom and Dad were good people. I had a lot of good influences in my life that made me be a good person. At least I hope I'm a good person. I try to be someone Mom and Dad would be proud of."

In a booklet she wrote about Hospice, Brenda wrote, "I used to send flowers to the funeral home, but years ago during the loss of my stepson, someone showed up to our door with a laundry basket of essential items: paper plates, plastic cups, trash bags, beverages, dish liquid, washing powder, napkins, and paper towels. Items I never knew we even needed until we needed them. Paper products are essential during this time. So, I have adopted this idea and now use it whenever we suffer the loss of a friend. I fill a laundry basket full of these essential items. We may also give restaurant gift cards to cover a dinner for an evening."

Brenda also wrote, "I was a Hospice nurse for a patient in a facility, and I asked the nurse on duty to medicate my patient. She said she didn't need it as she was sleeping, and the medications were PRN (as needed). I explained that she needed the medications. She said she can't justify giving her medications. I said it's called symptoms management. She said the patient will need to ask for the medication herself. I tried to educate the nurse, but she was offended and left the room. It's important to be polite but firm. I make no apologies when I am advocating for someone who needs me. I had to call the Hospice doctor, who in turn called the facility nurse who quickly and efficiently medicated the patient as requested. Let's face it, we're not here to make friends. If it takes rudeness to do what's right, I'll be rude."

***

The doing of good deeds is important. As a free person, you can choose to live your life as a good person or as a bad person. To be a good person, do good deeds. To be a bad person, do bad deeds. If you do good deeds, you will become good. If you do bad deeds, you will become bad. To become the person you want to be, act as if you already are that kind of person. Each of us chooses what kind of person we will become. To become a good person, do the things a good person does. To become a bad person, do the things a bad person does. The opportunity to take action to become the kind of person you want to be is yours.

Cover illustration for J.W. Gent.'s *The Valiant Scot*: A Retelling:
Public Domain Cover Illustration: William Wallace

Educate Yourself
Read Like a Wolf Eats
Be Excellent to Each Other
Books Then, Books Now, Books Forever

***

In this retelling, as in all my retellings, I have tried to make the work of literature accessible to modern readers who may lack some of the knowledge about mythology, religion, and history that the literary work's contemporary audience had.

Do you know a language other than English? If you do, I give you permission to translate this book, copyright your translation, publish or self-publish it, and keep all the royalties for yourself. (Do give me credit, of course, for the original retelling.)

I would like to see my retellings of classic literature used in schools, so I give permission to the country of Finland (and all other countries) to give copies of any or all of my retellings to all students forever. I also give permission to the state of Texas (and all other states) to give copies of this book to all students forever. I also give permission to all teachers to give copies of this book to all students forever.

Teachers need not actually teach my retellings. Teachers are welcome to give students copies of my eBooks as background material. For example, if they are teaching Homer's *Iliad* and *Odyssey*, teachers are welcome to give students copies of my *Virgil's* Aeneid: *A Retelling in Prose* and tell students, "Here's another ancient epic you may want to read in your spare time."

CAST OF CHARACTERS

SCOTS:

Robert Bruce. Earl of Carrick. Called "Earl of Huntingdon," although there were no Earls of Huntingdon from 1237-1377. Robert Bruce's life dates: 1274-1329. A good case can be made that Robert Bruce is the valiant Scot of the title.

Old Wallace

William Wallace

Peggy. Betrothed to William Wallace. Daughter to Sir John Graham.

Friar Gertrid

Sir John Graham. Friend to Old Wallace. Peg's father.

Supporters of Wallace:

John Comyn

Sir John Menteith

Gilbert de Grimsby

Lords:

Douglas

Macbeth

Wintersdale

General

Rugecrosse — Herald

ENGLISH:

Edward I. King Edward I of England (reigned 1272-1307, born 1239).

Queen Eleanor of Castile

Sebastian. Nephew to Queen

Lords:

Beaumont

Sir Robert de Clifford

Sir Henry de Percy. Called "Earl of Northumberland" — but that title was not created until 1377.

Earl of Hertford
Earl of Hereford
Ambassadors to Scots:

Glascot
Mountford

Commissioners ruling over Scotland:

Sir William Hazelrigg
Sir Thomas Selby
Thorne

Young Selby
Sir Jeffrey Wiseacres J.P. [Justice of the Peace]
Bolt. Wiseacres' Clerk.
Gallants, Messengers, Heralds, English Soldiers, Scottish Soldiers, Prince Edward.

NOTA BENE:

King Edward I

Reigned 1272-1307, born 1239. Known as Edward Longshanks because of his tallness, King Edward I fought and defeated the Welsh chieftains, and he made his eldest son the Prince of Wales. He won victories against the Scots, and he brought the coronation stone from Scone to Westminster.

Sir William Wallace

Sir William Wallace is one of the great heroes of Scotland.

He was Guardian of the Kingdom of Scotland (the Second Interregnum) from 1297-1298. Preceding him was John Balliol, King of the Scots, and following him was Robert the Bruce, King of the Scots.

Sir William Wallace (c. 1270 to 23 August 1305) was one of the leaders of the First War of Scottish Independence (1296-1328).

In May 1297, he and a small band of men burned Lanark and killed its sheriff.

He and Andrew Moray defeated the English at the Battle of Stirling Bridge in September 1297. A few months later, he was knighted.

Following that important victory, he became Guardian of the Scottish Kingdom. He was defeated at the Battle of Falkirk in July 1298 and resigned as Guardian of the Kingdom of Scotland in December.

He lived an outlaw's life until he was captured in August 1305 at Robroyston, near Glasgow. King Edward I of England declared him guilty of high treason and had him hung, drawn, and quartered on 23 August 1305.

Blind Harry wrote a 15th-century epic poem about him, and Jane Porter wrote about him in her 1810 historical novel titled *The Scottish Chiefs*. Sir Walter Scott also wrote about him in *Exploits and Death of William Wallace, the "Hero of Scotland."*

Mel Gibson played William Wallace in the 1995 film *Braveheart*. The film won a Best Picture Oscar, and Mel Gibson won an Oscar for Best Director.

Robert the Bruce

Robert the Bruce was King of Scots from 25 March 1306 until his death on 7 June 1329. He was born on 11 July 1274. Preceding him as King was John Balliol. In between these kings, William Wallace served as Guardian of the Scottish Kingdom.

A renowned warrior and Scottish hero, Robert the Bruce supported William Wallace in his rebellion against King Edward I of England.

Following the events of this play, Robert the Bruce fought England, and King Edward III of England renounced all claims to sovereignty over Scotland in the 1328 Treaty of Edinburgh–Northampton.

History

We don't read Elizabethan, Jacobean, or Carolinian historical plays and expect historical accuracy.

Playwrights feel free to change facts to suit their needs.

William Wallace did not marry the daughter of Sir John Graham.

Robert Bruce did not fight at the Battle of Falkirk, either for or against Scotland.

Dates

King Edward I participated in the Ninth Crusade in 1281-82.

In 1291, the Crusades ended when Acre, the last Christian stronghold in the Holy Land, fell. King Edward I was not present, but he gave up his plans for participating in another Crusade.

On 11 September 1297, the Scots, led by William Wallace and Andrew Moray, decisively defeated the English at the Battle of Stirling Bridge.

On 22 July 1298, the English decisively defeated the Scots at the Battle of Falkirk.

Following the defeat at the Battle of Falkirk, William Wallace lived an outlaw's life until he was captured in August 1305 at Robroyston, near Glasgow.

William Wallace was declared guilty of high treason.

Treason is disloyalty, and high treason is disloyalty against one's king. An example of treason is waging war against the king.

On 23 August 1305, King Edward I of England had William Wallace hung, drawn, and quartered.

William Wallace's answer to the charge of treason was, "I could not be a traitor to Edward, for I was never his subject."

The Valiant Scot was first performed in 1637.

SCOTTISH DIALECT

Here are some useful resources:

Dictionary of the Scots Language

https://dsl.ac.uk

Glossary of Scottish Slang and Jargon

https://en.wiktionary.org/wiki/
Appendix:Glossary_of_Scottish_slang_and_jargon

EDITIONS WITH NOTES

George F. Byers, editor

The Valiant Scot, by J.W.: A Critical Edition. George F. Byers, editor. New York: Garland Pub., 1980. Print.

Patricia A. Griffin, editor, aka Pat Griffin

As a student at Sheffield Hallam University, Patricia A. Griffin edited the play. Her edition is the first modern-spelling edition.

J. W. Gent. THE VALIANT SCOT. Editor: Patricia A. Griffin. Sheffield Hallam University. 2007. PDF.

Patricia A. Griffin's edition can be found here:

https://extra.shu.ac.uk/emls/iemls/renplays/valiantscot/contents.htm

Here is a list of Sheffield Hallam University student editions (and links to those editions):

https://extra.shu.ac.uk/emls/iemls/resources.html

The Society of This Play

In this society, a person of higher rank would use "thou," "thee," "thine," and "thy" when referring to a person of lower rank. (These terms were also used affectionately and between equals.) A person of lower rank would use "you" and "your" when referring to a person of higher rank.

"Sirrah" was a title used to address someone of a social rank inferior to the speaker. Friends, however, could use it to refer to each other.

The word "wench" in Ben Jonson's time was not necessarily negative. It was often used affectionately.

A "gossip" is a friend or companion or neighbor.

The word "cousin" can mean 1) relative (not necessarily what we call a cousin today), or 2) friend.

CHAPTER 1

— 1.1 —

Sir William Hazelrigg, Sir Thomas Selby, Thorne, and Sir Jeffrey Wiseacres talked together in a council chamber in the castle of Lanark in Scotland.

Hazelrigg, Selby, and Thorne were English, but they were Commissioners ruling over Scotland.

King Edward I of England had defeated the Scottish forces in 1296. King John Balliol of Scotland abdicated and was imprisoned in the Tower of London before going into exile in France.

"Fellow colleagues!" Thorne said. "Since it has pleased our king, renowned Edward, of his special favor to enclose us in this height of eminence and make us rulers over Scotland, let's show ourselves worthy of the dignities conferred upon us."

"That's not by leniency for notwithstanding that the armèd hand of war has made them ours, they are a nation haughty and proud and full of spleen and hot temper and must be managed with stricter and tighter reins and rougher bits," Sir Thomas Selby said.

Sir Thomas Selby had likened Scotland to a hot-tempered horse that needed to be controlled.

Reins and bits are used to control horses.

Thorne said:

"Alas, I find them easy, tractable, and mild. Authority may, with a slender twine, hold in the strongest head. Why then does tyranny need to use a rein or bit? By this all doubts and fears are cleared.

"It is always better to be loved than feared. And by your leave, Sir Thomas, we have good reason to defend our own: our fellow citizens and those entrusted to us."

If the Scots were to recognize King Edward I of England as their legitimate ruler, they would not rebel. Their loyalty to England would be a good defence for England and for Scotland: English armies and Scottish armies would have no need to fight each other.

The other Englishmen preferred to be feared rather than loved: They believed that being feared was more profitable.

Sir Thomas Selby began, "You are as clear of danger and as free from foes and fears —"

Sir William Hazelrigg interrupted:

"— as he who holds a hungry wolf by the ears.

"The principles are true. Trust not thy wife with secrets, nor thy vassal with thy life. Sound example proves it and private policy confirms it. I could urge reason why, show cause wherefore, and speak to purpose whereby, but my betters are in place.

"I know them to be pregnant and full of ideas, and I know that a ready intelligence is worth all."

"For our own safety then, and for England's honor, let us not lose what our king won with hard effort," Sir Thomas Selby said.

Sir William Hazelrigg said:

"For that reason we have called this solemn meeting, to which we have summoned some people.

"Chiefly we have summoned Old Wallace, the late Sheriff of Ayr. Although the King has conferred that office on me, the haughty Scot thinks much to tender and offer up."

Old Wallace wanted to offer the office to his son eventually.

Sir William Hazelrigg continued:

"Observe Old Wallace's insolence."

Old Wallace entered the scene and took his place. He believed that his place was the seat for the Sheriff of Ayr.

"Presumptuous groom," Sir Thomas Selby said. "This is a seat for eagles and not for haggards."

A groom is a servant.

A haggard is 1) literally, a wild adult hawk, or one caught as an adult and therefore difficult to train, or 2) figuratively, a wild, hard-to-control person.

Old Wallace replied, "Selby, it is a seat that I, and my grandfather's grandfather, have enjoyed and held with worship — with distinction — and, until King Edward's hand will remove me from it, Old Wallace will still continue to possess it."

"Proud Wallace dares not!" Sir Thomas Selby said.

Old Wallace replied to Sir Thomas Selby, sometimes referring to both him and himself in the third person:

"Selby! Wallace both dares and does, and must, and will, although he is a subject to King Edward.

"I'm Selby's equal both in birth and place — in social rank and position.

"Although in my office — my position as Sheriff of Ayr — King Edward joined you with me, he never made you ruler over me."

"You'll find he did!" Sir William Hazelrigg said. "Read that commission and tell me then if Selby or you yourself is Sheriff of Ayr."

He handed Old Wallace the commission, and Old Wallace read it.

"To what my King commands I humbly bend, resigning on my knee both staff and office," Old Wallace said.

Sir Thomas Selby said:

"—which thus Selby breaks over thy head."

He snapped the staff — a symbol of office — over Old Wallace's head.

Sir Thomas Selby continued:

"And now, proud Sir, acknowledge Selby to be your ruler, and with your place resign your castle and your lands."

Old Wallace said:

"That's not inserted in your commission.

"What King Edward has given to you, I surrender.

"As for my lands, they're still my own. They were purchased with the sweat of my dear ancestors, and before I lose a pole, a foot, aye, or the smallest turf a silly — an innocent — lark may build a nest on, I'll lose my life."

A pole is a unit of measurement: 5.5 yards.

"It's your own choice," Sir Thomas Selby said. "You can lose either your lands or your life, or you can lose both."

"Or I can lose neither," Old Wallace said. "Royal Edward's mercy sits above Selby's malice and evil."

"Surly groom," Sir Thomas Selby said. "Mercy's for subjects. By what evidence, charter, or service do you hold your land?"

"Evidence" is a deed of title. "Charter" is a deed of conveyance of property. "To hold in service" means to be a tenant.

Old Wallace said:

"Selby, by none.

"That title that I had, I have given to my son, a boy of that proud temper that should he hear thy insolent demand would pluck thee from thy seat and lay thy head as a satisfaction — a tribute — at his father's feet.

"But the heavens forbid it.

"Selby, thus it stands. Thou have my office, and my son has my lands."

"He must show how he holds them," Sir Thomas Selby said.

Old Wallace said:

"So he can, and, Selby, he will show sufficient evidence — my sword, my dear father's sword, and my grandfather's sword.

"He wears good evidence about him, Selby, and he will upon the least occasion — the least opportunity — both show and prove it lawful."

Sir William Hazelrigg said, "If the sword is your best plea, you have but a naked title, and, by our authority, we here command that you and your son appear at our next general meeting to bring in your surrender of your lands, or undergo the penalty of traitors."

An unsheathed sword is a "naked" weapon. A naked title is one that lacks any legal force.

The penalty of traitors was death.

Old Wallace and his son, William Wallace, would be forced to surrender their lands or be executed as traitors.

Sir John Graham entered the scene. He was a Scotsman who was a friend to Old Wallace, and he had a daughter named Peggy who was betrothed to William Wallace.

He said to Sir William Hazelrigg, Thorne, and Sir Thomas Selby:

"Oh, you, the patrons of poor injured subjects, give Graham justice.

"Selby's riotous son, assisted by a crew of dissolute men, has stolen my only daughter and intends a violent rape or, which more cuts my soul, a forced marriage."

Sir Thomas Selby said:

"Inconsiderate — thoughtless — fool!

"The boy affects her — he wants her — and, with my consent, he intends a lawful marriage. It is a favor her betters sue for."

In other words: According to Sir Thomas Selby, other women who are better than Sir John Graham's daughter would love to be married to Selby's son.

Sir John Graham said, "Oh, let them — my daughter and your son — hate each other. My flesh and blood shall never enter league and covenant, nor hold alliance and union, with a man who hates my country."

Sir Thomas Selby said:

"Rest your thoughts!

"He has her. If he likes her, he shall wed her, and, Graham, as a dowry, he shall enjoy thy present estate, revenues, goods, and lands.

"Fret out thy soul, he shall enjoy them."

In other words: All your possessions shall be confiscated and given to my son as a dowry to marry your daughter. Go ahead and fret and worry: What I say will happen will in fact happen.

"He shall marry my daughter?" Sir John Graham asked.

Sir Thomas Selby said:

"Aye, sir, he shall!

"It's the highest favor conquest can afford, for a slave to join alliance with his Lord."

He then said to Old Wallace:

"And Wallace, see that you make immediate surrender of your lands, or else look for storms."

Sir Jeffrey Wiseacres, an English Justice of the Peace, said, "So say I, too, and it is not the least part of policy, neither."

Policy is political craftiness: Give up your lands so you don't have to give up your life. Sir Jeffrey Wiseacres regarded it as the politic thing to do: the best result that can come out of this situation.

Old Wallace said, "Will have my lands!"

The subject of the sentence may be "I."

Sir William Hazelrigg, Sir Thomas Selby, Thorne, and Sir Jeffrey Wiseacres exited.

Sir John Graham said, "They will force me to give a dowry. This is misery decreed above comparison."

"Complain to King Edward," Old Wallace said.

Sir John Graham said, using the royal plural for King Edward I:

"The king, alas, have heard a story how the subtle fox, having stolen a lamb, the family of sheep drew up a petition and, with full consent, delivered it to the lion. He, employed about earnest and more serious business, appointed the bear to be commissioner and take up this bloody difference: this quarrel involving bloodshed. The bear chose and impaneled a partial — as opposed to impartial — jury consisting all of wolves. They chose the fox to be their foreman. They consulted and found the sheepish nation guilty and, with general breath, cast votes and convicted, judged, condemned, and sentenced all to death."

In other words: The fox stole a lamb but ended up being its own judge and condemning a nation of sheep to be slaughtered.

Also in other words: King Edward I is busy with other matters, and the people who are committing crimes in Scotland are the same people who judge the people who commit crimes in Scotland.

"Men should have souls," Old Wallace said.

Sir John Graham said:

"But tyrants, being no men, have consequently none.

"Complaints made by slaves are like prayers made over dead men's graves: They are neither heard, nor pitied.

"Heaven has imposed a curse that sufferance — patient endurance — in time may cure, and complaints do make worse."

Old Wallace said:

"Then, as it is, let's bear it. Win heaven to friend.

"He — God — Who begins, knows when and how to end."

God has no beginning, and God began — created — the universe.

Young Selby and other gallants were guarding Peggy on a street in the town of Lanark. Peggy was betrothed to William Wallace, but Sir Thomas Selby's son — Young Selby — wanted to marry her.

Gallants were fashionable young gentlemen who carried swords.

Young Selby said:

"Mask her!

"Come, Peg, hide your Scottish face."

Brides in England were customarily masked.

Peggy said with a heavy Scottish accent, "Why shild I hayd my Scottish feace? My Scottish feace is as gude as your English feace. 'Tis a true Scottish feace."

[Why should I hide my Scottish face? My Scottish face is as good as your English face. It is a true Scottish face.]

Peggy may have been using Scottish dialect as an act of pride in her heritage and as an act of defiance against the English. In this play, characters such as William Wallace can speak with or without a Scottish dialect as suits their purposes.

"I know it is, sweet Peggy," Young Selby said. "And because it is not a picture for every painter to draw forth, let this curtain be pinned before it."

In this society, curtains were hung in front of valuable paintings to protect them when they were not being viewed.

Peggy said:

"Hang yare flee-flaps! No Scottish woman is ashamed of that luke that the master painter abuise gives her. Whare mun I gangand now? Fay! Fay! Fay! What losel am I, that am hurrand thus, to and fra with swords and wapins? Whay mun back'erd men go fencing and florishing about me? Am I yare May-game?"

[Hang your fly-cloths! No Scottish woman is ashamed of that look that the master painter God above gives her. Where must I go walking now? Foe! Foe! Foe! What scoundrel am I, who is hurried like this, to and fro with swords and weapons? Why must backward, perverse men go fencing and flourishing their weapons about me? Am I your May-game?]

"Gangand" [gan = go, gang = go on foot] means "go walking."

"—ang" also can mean "—ing," and so "ganging" can mean "going."

"Fa" and "fay" can mean "foe, enemy."

"Fey" and "fay" can mean "doomed to die."

"Fay" can mean "religious faith."

"Fay" can mean "fie," aka "bah."

In the spring, people would dance around a May pole and engage in other games.

"No, Peggy," Young Selby said. "Thou are my prisoner, but here's thy jail."

Peggy said, "Are you my jailor? What kin bin you to the hangman? Sent you? Whare's he? Wha is that foul loon amang you, that mun be my hangman?"

[Are you my jailor? What relative are you to the hangman? Who sent you? Where is he? Who is that worthless rogue among you, that loon who must be my hangman?]

"Here's no man here who is your hangman, or your jailor," Young Selby replied.

"Wha' then be you?" Peggy asked.

[Who then are you?]

"Your friends who hold you only in bonds of love," Young Selby answered.

Peggy said, "I reckand mickle your 'luife.' Fie upon such luife. Thee owd felon thief, luifand the true-man's siller as you luifand me. I'd rather be a Scotchman's whore than an Englishman's wife and be dreave to the kirk with helters."

[I reckon that your "love" is much. Bah upon such love. Thou old felon thief, thou are loving the trustworthy man's silver as much as you are loving me. I'd rather be a Scotchman's whore than an Englishman's wife and be driven to the church with halters."]

One reason to marry Peggy other than sex was to get a dowry from her father. The true — trustworthy — man was her father.

Halters are used to control animals.

English brides were led to the church by people holding the bride's arms. It was if they were taking the bride to the church by force.

The custom of carrying the bride across the threshold dates back to the Romans as a kind of reference to the Rape of the Sabine Women. When Rome was founded, the first Romans were mostly men. They needed wives, so they invited the Sabines to a feast and when a signal was given, they seized the Sabine women. This is marriage by capture.

The phrase "to rape" means 1) to forcibly seize and abduct, and 2) to sexually violate.

"Tell me what proud Scot loves thee?" Young Selby asked. "What Scot dares to touch thee, now thou are Selby's?"

Peggy said, "Hang thee! Hang thee, foul meazel'd loon! What Scotchman dares, guif! If my luif understood my case, on God's dear earth thou sud no fader gange. As butchers' kie to the ground, he sud thou bang!"

[Hang yourself! Hang yourself, you foul infected (measled) loon! What Scotchman dares, fool! If my love understood my situation, on God's dear earth thou should no further go on foot. As butchers strike cattle and they fall to the ground, he would violently strike thee down.]

"All mildness is in vain," the second gallant advised Young Selby. "Take some rough course of action."

"To the church!" Young Selby said. "Let's go! I'll marry her there by force."

"Away with her!" the first gallant said. "Let's take her away!"

William Wallace and his supporters Comyn and Menteith entered the scene.

Peggy ran to William Wallace, her betrothed.

"Yonder's Wallace, and his crue," the second gallant said.

The word "crue" means 1) crew, followers, 2) pigsty, and/or 3) trap for fish.

"The devil and his dam, it is," Young Selby said. "Don't budge."

Peggy said to William Wallace, "Oh, my luife! These southern carles mickle wrang 'gainst me work, and now wad force me gang until the kirk and marry Selby. Wallace, my jo, not I!"

[Oh, my love! These southern churls much wrong work against me, and now they would force me to walk to the church and marry Selby. Wallace, my lover, not I!]

"Unhand that beauteous prize, proud slave!" Young Selby said to William Wallace. "It is mine!"

"You call me a slave?" William Wallace said. "Thou are a villain, Young Selby!"

"Are you so brave?" Young Selby asked.

"Look after my wench," William Wallace said to his supporters.

In this society, the word "wench" was often used affectionately and not as an insult.

"Kill them!" Comyn and Menteith replied.

"We are no stars, to die by dozens," William Wallace said to Young Selby.

"Stars" are falling stars (meteors). On 28 October 1602, a spectacular meteor shower occurred over Britain.

Young Selby told his supporters:

"Stay back!"

He then said to William Wallace:

"The quarrel's mine, and if one single Scot — the proudest of your swarm of followers — dares answer me, step forth!"

"Your first man, I am, Sir!" William Wallace said.

He was very willing to fight Young Selby. There was no need for one of his followers to do that.

Young Selby said:

"Listen, gentlemen.

"Don't let so slight a shower that yet lies hidden and wrapped in one poor cloud be by rough winds (raised up by you) dispersed into a general storm. Quick lightning shoots forth already to many eyes of Scots and English.

"But your absence will allay those fires that otherwise must kindle.

"Get yourself then away and take shelter in yonder tavern."

He wanted everyone other than William Wallace and himself to leave, lest a general brawl should break out.

This was good thinking on Young Selby's part.

"Agreed," the gallants said.

"Look after my Peggy!" William Wallace said.

Peggy, Comyn, Menteith, and the gallants exited.

"Guard my love!" Young Selby said. "He and I will only exchange cold words."

He meant that William Wallace and he would only talk and not fight.

"Now, sir!" William Wallace said. "What are your cold words?"

"This Scottish lass, I love her," Young Selby said.

"Is that all?" William Wallace asked.

"Yes!" Young Selby said.

"I love her, too," William Wallace said. "Can any words more cold strike your heart?"

"Is she your wife?" Young Selby asked.

"No," William Wallace said.

"Is she your whore?" Young Selby asked.

"No!" William Wallace said. "She is neither my wife nor my whore."

"She gangs with me, then," Young Selby said.

"Gangs" is Scottish dialect for "goes."

"Only the dewle — the devil and the duel — knows whither she goes," William Wallace said. "If you can win her, wear her. She's wholly mine."

Playwrights at this time were often bawdy. "Wholly" may be a pun on "hole": vagina.

He wanted to fight a duel to determine who would wed Peggy.

"If you can win her, wear her" means "if you can win the duel and so win her, marry her and take her to bed."

Clothing can keep people warm, and wives can keep husbands warm.

A phrase from the porn-movie industry may be relevant here: meat puppet.

Reacting to the statement, "She's wholly mine," Young Selby asked, "Is she?"

"She is!" William Wallace said. "Our lasses are not English common. I'm right Scottish bred — until death, stick to a woman."

The common was land common to all: land where anyone could graze animals.

"And to the death thou shall," Young Selby said. "No more but death shall thou bear from me, Scot."

"When shall we fight?" William Wallace asked.

"Instantly," Young Selby said. "Make your choice, sir, of your weapon, time, and place."

The person who was challenged could choose the duel's weapons, time, and place.

"This whinyard — this sword — shall be my weapon," William Wallace said.

"This?" Young Selby asked.

William Wallace and Young Selby held their swords against each other's to see if their length was equal. A person with a longer sword would have an advantage in a duel.

Their swords were equal in length.

William Wallace said:

"Our swords do now agree, and they are of one length and full measure.

"If we must have surgeons tomorrow, why shouldn't we have them now, although they need not be as good as the surgeons needed tomorrow?

"It is the English fashion to swagger it out and then drink, and then fight and kill in cold blood, having slept soundly all night, and often the seconds fall all gashed when home, in whole and uninjured skins, come the principal duelists.

"So, about words, the lawyer wrangling stands,

"And loses in the meantime his client's lands."

The seconds are supporters and assistants during the duel.

William Wallace was insulting the English fashion of fighting: The English swagger and drink and sleep and then "kill" with cold-blooded words and mean-spirited gossip.

Often, the people who get hurt are those who are not directly involved in the quarrel.

Also according to William Wallace, people who fight with words are likely to lose what they are fighting for.

William Wallace sounded as if he were describing English courtiers.

According to William Wallace's words, the English fashion of dueling sheds more "blood" with words than with swords.

"Do thou teach me fencing, too, in thy own school?" Young Selby said. "I'll beat thee or be beaten; one draws short breath."

One of them would breathe for only a short time longer.

"I feel no sickness," William Wallace said.

"Yet thou are near thy death," Young Selby said.

They fought.

The two English gallants and the Scottish Comyn and Menteith returned.

Wallace lost his weapon in the duel.

"At it so hotly!" the first gallant said.

"Kill him!" the second gallant said. "It is fair!"

"That would be an inglorious conquest!" Young Selby said. "For King Edward's crown, I'd trample on no enemy were he down."

Young Selby handed Wallace's sword to him and said, "There! If thou are well and unwounded, depart."

This was a magnanimous gesture on Young Selby's part.

If William Wallace left now, Young Selby would win the duel and he would win and wear Peggy.

William Wallace said, "I'll die, or in thy heat's blood wash away this infamy."

They fought, and Wallace struck Selby with a fatal blow.

"May God have mercy on my soul!" Young Selby said.

He died.

"He's slain!" Comyn said.

"Let's get away!" Menteith said.

"Shift for yourselves," William Wallace said. "It will prove to be a stormy day."

Young Selby's father, Sir Thomas Selby, would want to get revenge.

All exited, leaving Young Selby's corpse behind.

<h1 style="text-align:center">— 1.3. —</h1>

Someone yelled, "Murder! Murder!"

Sir Thomas Selby, Thorne, Sir William Hazelrigg, Peggy, and the two gallants entered the scene.

"Search!" the two gallants shouted. "Call for surgeons! Follow the murderer!"

Peggy said, "Woe is me! Ligs my luife on the cawd ground? Let me come kiss his frosty mouth."

[Woe is me! My love lies on the cold ground? Let me come kiss his frosty mouth.]

"What Scot is it?" Sir Thomas Selby asked.

"Oh!" the two gallants said, looking at the corpse's face. "It is Young Selby!"

"He's my son!" Sir Thomas Selby said. "Who slew him?"

"That fatal hand of William Wallace," the first gallant said.

"Follow the villain!" Sir Thomas Selby said.

Peggy said, "I'z jocund and well now."

[I'm happy and well now.]

"Lay a fast hold upon her!" Sir William Hazelrigg said.

Peggy said, "Hang me! I reck not!'

[Hang me! I don't care!]

"Away with her to prison!" Thorne said. "Take her to prison."

Everyone exited.

<h1 style="text-align:center">— 1.4. —</h1>

King Edward I, Queen Eleanor, Percy, Beaumont, Grimsby, Prince Edward, Sebastian, and Robert Bruce met together in the English court.

Percy and Beaumont were English lords. Percy was a lord of the north: the Earl of Northumberland.

Grimsby and Robert Bruce were Scots who at this time supported King Edward I. Robert Bruce owned much land in England. He was hopeful that King Edward I would help him achieve the Scottish crown and make him King of Scots.

Sebastian was nephew to Queen Eleanor.

King Edward I said, "Not all the blood and treasure we have spent like zealous prodigals in Palestine goes half as near our heart as that which the proud King of France, knowing our merit, deprives us of and bars us from what is our due."

The parable of the Prodigal Son is told in Luke 15:11-32.

France was a Scottish ally, but this conflict was over the Duchy of Gascony, which King Phillip IV of France had confiscated. Before the King of France did that, the Duchy of Gascony was held in personal union with the Kingdom of England. This means that the Duchy of Gascony and the Kingdom of England had the same ruler — Edward I — but different laws.

"The King of France dares not do that," Percy said.

"Yes, he does," King Edward I said.

"Then it was not demanded," Percy said.

Grimsby, who had spoken as an ambassador from England to the King of France, said, "What! Not demanded? Does the bold Lord Percy think that Grimsby dares not — when lawfully employed — demand?"

He would make demands as needed while on a lawful errand such as the one that King Edward I had sent him on.

"But not command," Percy said.

"Yes!" Grimsby said. "Command, Percy."

He could and would make — and had made — commands when commands were needed.

Percy replied, "Grimsby, thou can do well in garrison, wear chamois for a grace, project and make schemes for blood, make eight days to one week, turn executioner and, hangman like, send fifty in one morning to die and feed the crows, and live upon dead pay."

Garrison officers are behind-the-battle-lines officers. According to Percy, Grimsby does well when he is not fighting.

Soldiers joked that to receive one week's pay, they had to work eight days. The extra day's wages would be kept by their officer.

Some commanders would collect for themselves the wages of soldiers who were dead.

Grimsby had been insulted.

Grimsby said, "He's a man worse than dead who —"

Percy began, "Stop thy throat or —"

"What?" Grimsby interrupted.

Percy finished, "— I'll cut it!"

"Cut-throat!" Grimsby said.

"It is a trade by which few prosper, and yet thou are a made man because of it," Percy said.

Grimsby said, "A man as good as —"

Percy interrupted, "— a hangman!"

"A foul blot lies in your throat!" Grimsby said.

These were fighting words that could result in a duel.

"Thy foul mouth!" Percy said. "Wash it, Scot!"

"In Percy's blood I'll wash it!" Grimsby said.

King Edward I said:

"Grimsby, you lean too hard upon our sufferance and toleration.

"And noble Percy, who are our honored second — our primary advisor — in all inward combats, thou have too many worthy parts of man to throw thyself on this unequal hazard.

"Grimsby, thou stand so much degreed below him, both in your descent and your eminent quality, aka exalted rank. The many favors we have graced thee with blush to have been conferred upon a man no better tempered."

According to King Edward I, Grimsby should control himself better.

King Edward I did not want the two men to fight. For one thing, the two men were not social equals. Percy ranked higher in this society than Grimsby did.

A man of a higher social class could decline to fight a man of a lower social class. Knights did not fight peasants in duels.

Wanting to change the subject of conversation away from criticism of his countryman, Robert Bruce began, "May it please my Sovereign to confirm his grant — his promise — touching and concerning —"

King Edward I finished the sentence for him: "— the crown of Scotland."

He then said:

"Some other time.

"Grimsby, thou have raised a storm that showers of blood can hardly lay to rest."

Grimsby said:

"Dread Liege, if all the youthful blood that I have spent and the wealthy honors that my sword has won, waving the Christian standard in the face of the proud pagan in the Holy Land, merit the name of hangman, then Grimsby casts them and himself at royal Edward's feet.

"And, like an outworn soldier, he humbly begs no pension" — he said to himself, "But look out, Percy" — "nor yet any office except leave — permission — to leave the Court, and rich in stars to lose more blood or win more worth in wars."

In this society, people believed that stars influenced one's fortune in life. Stars could be lucky or unlucky. People believed in astrology.

King Edward I replied:

"We will not lose thee, Grimsby."

He still wanted Grimsby to be a member of his court.

He then began:

"Valiant Percy, if love in us, or loyalty in you, has any power —"

Knowing that the king wanted him to make peace with Grimsby, Percy said, "My sovereign's pleasure sits above my private passions."

"Passions" are strong emotions.

King Edward I said, "Then join hands, our subjects both, the natives of two lands."

The two lands, of course, were England (Percy) and Scotland (Grimsby).

"Are we friends, Grimsby?" Percy asked.

Grimsby and Percy shook hands.

Grimsby said to himself, "We are friends in show, but in my breast revenge lies waiting in ambush."

He was still angry at Percy.

Robert Bruce began, "Gracious liege —"

King Edward I said:

"Thou are no musician, Bruce. Thou keep false time."

Using the royal plural, he said:

"We strike a bloody lachrymae — a sad tune — to France and thou keep time to a Scotch jig to arms."

Scot jigs are lively tunes that are not suitable to be played as martial music.

"Edward will be more kind to Christians," Queen Eleanor said.

The French were Catholics.

King Edward I said:

"Let Christians be more honest then, to Edward, in expedition of this holy war."

England and the Netherlands had joined with Catholic France in a grand alliance against Spain. King Edward I was unhappy with the French performance in this alliance. An English army had fought to ensure the security of France, and France was not acknowledging any debt for that military aid.

King Edward I continued:

"When the King of France in person was enjoined to march, to work his safety we engaged our own soldiers.

"We cashiered — paid off — his fainting soldiers and, on promise of so much gold at our return, we supplied English soldiers to carry the French designs ourself. Yes, we carried out the French plans.

"And is our love and loss of blood, half of which at least would have dropped out of French bosoms, quittant with owe none? Is it a debt cancelled with no payment?"

England had expected payment for its military expenses.

King Edward I continued:

"Pillage and play the freebooter for more."

This was part of the quarrel with the King of France: France was refusing to pay money owed to England. One way for England to get the money back — and more — would be to pillage France.

"Freebooters" are pirates and other lawbreakers.

Sir William Hazelrigg entered the scene.

"What is the news?" King Edward I asked.

"Dread sovereign, Scotland is infected with a most dangerous surfeit: a sickness resulting from excess," Sir William Hazelrigg said. "It breaks out in strong rebellion."

"This is your kingdom rebelling, Bruce," King Edward I said.

"I have no hand in it, though," Robert Bruce said.

"Thou should have no head, if we did but think you had a hand in it," King Edward I said. "Who is the chief of the rebels?"

"A man named Wallace," Sir William Hazelrigg said. "He is a fellow meanly and poorly bred but spirited above belief."

King Edward I dismissed William Wallace:

"Some needy borderer."

A borderer is someone living on or near borders — in this case, the border of Scotland and England.

King Edward I asked:

"How is our bosom parted?"

The king represented the commonwealth. Any rebellion was a division of the commonwealth and therefore of the king.

King Edward I believed that he had the authority to rule Scotland.

King Edward I continued:

"Is their power — their army — of any strength?

"Bruce, levy soldiers for an army to fight in France. If we but thought thee touched and implicated in the Scottish rebellion ...."

He did not finish his sentence but instead said:

"Warlike Percy, Beaumont, and Sebastian, fetch him — William Wallace — in, or with a second and more fatal conquest, ruin that stubborn nation."

King Edward I had already defeated Scotland once. He was threatening to defeat Scotland more strongly a second time.

Queen Eleanor said, "Gracious Edward, although war has made them subjects, heaven defend — heaven forbid — that subjects should make them vassals."

Subjects rank higher than vassals. Citizens are more productive than slaves, who are more servile.

King Edward I replied:

"We conceit — we understand — you.

"If any officer of ours transgresses and goes beyond our will, or goes beyond his boundaries that are pre-fixed, we'll have his head.

"He who seeks to make our free subjects his slaves depraves and corrupts our high worth."

"We do not seek to do that," Sir William Hazelrigg said.

"See to it that we find no transgression of our will," King Edward I said.

Queen Eleanor said:

"Let Eleanor win so much favor as to march along with you.

"Although the Scots are conquered, alas, we are neighbors of one clime, and we live like them subject to change and time."

The two countries had the same climate and land: They were on the island of Britain.

Grimsby said, "Royal Edward, although Wallace and some spleenful dissolutes, wronged with the yoke of bondage, cast it off, don't let the whole land suffer."

In other words: Although a few Scots are rebels, don't make all of Scotland suffer for their actions.

King Edward I said:

"Nor do we wish all of Scotland to suffer, Grimsby.

"Should the Fates just turn the Wheel of Fortune, we might with them exchange states — conditions — and we would be Scotland's subjects.

"But if rebellion should stop and then kneel,

"We'll wear soft mercy and cast off rough steel."

The Fates are goddesses who influence human life. They can give good fates or bad fates.

The Wheel of Fortune turns, and those who are at the top go to the bottom, and those who are at the bottom go to the top.

Grimsby said, "I'll undertake the mission."

Apparently, he would meet with William Wallace and try to stop the rebellion.

King Edward I said:

"Let messengers be sent to question the proud rebel, and if Grimsby fails in his plot, Northumberland and Clifford shall second him in arms."

Percy was the Earl of Northumberland.

King Edward I continued:

"So slight a foe must not detain us from our French designs.

"Our queen has all our breast and all our confidence, and although we might, justly perhaps, confine your liberty, Bruce, we enlarge it, giving you command in our French wars.

"Observe Bruce nearly and closely, lords. I have read this maxim in state policy: '*Be sure to wear thy danger in thy eye.*'"

In other words: Keep a close eye on your enemies.

King Edward I continued:

"France lights a comet, Scotland's a blazing star,

"Both seek for blood. We'll quench them both with war."

Comets and falling stars were omens: Wars were coming.

Everyone exited.

Robert Bruce would command the English army in France.

Grimsby would go to Scotland and try to persuade William Wallace to stop rebelling, or he would capture him and so stop his rebellion against King Edward I.

William Wallace, Comyn, and Menteith spoke together in the Scottish camp. William Wallace wanted to rescue his betrothed, Peggy, from the Englishmen who kept her prisoner in the castle of Lanark.

"Please, good Wallace!" Comyn pleaded.

"May ill happen to the soul of any man who speaks about goodness, thinks about goodness, or meditates about any goodness more than how to free imprisoned Peg," William Wallace replied.

Menteith said, "But hear me —"

"Lanark Castle wears only a slender bolt of brick," William Wallace said.

He was likening the castle's brick wall to a bolt of thin cloth.

Comyn said, "He's turned mad!"

He knew that rescuing Peggy would be difficult.

William Wallace said, "And say the moat is fifty fathoms deep, fifty times fifty, say it reaches all the way through to hell, Wallace will swim it!"

"Swim it?" Comyn said. "Yes! So will thou thrust an ox into an eggshell and roast it by moonshine. But why should Wallace do that?"

The Moon is "Luna," cognate with the word "lunatic."

William Wallace said, "Why should proud Selby, although his forward — his arrogant — son was justly slain, imprison Peg? Poor lamb, she is no murderer."

"In my conscience, she never drew a weapon in anger in her life," Comyn said.

Menteith said, "Not at sharp, I think, but by your leave, it is thought she has practiced in private, put Wallace to foil and made him lie at his hanging ward, many a time and often."

Hanging wards are defensive moves.

Peggy had not used sharp weapons, but people thought that she had practiced fencing using foils — blunted swords — and that she was so good that she had put William Wallace on the defensive many times.

The words can be interpreted bawdily. Peggy had often combatted William Wallace's "sword" and made it hang down, no longer erect. At such times,

William Wallace was foiled — his "sword" was blunted — and he would lie down and sleep.

Old Wallace and Sir John Graham entered the scene. They were the fathers of William Wallace and of Peggy, respectively.

"Where's my son?" Old Wallace asked.

"With Peggy, father," his son, William Wallace, answered. "Manacles of grief hang heavy on my senses."

"Shake them off!" Old Wallace said. "Show thyself worthy of him whom thou call father, or Peggy dies."

In other words: If William Wallace were to allow Peggy to remain a prisoner, she would die. Rescue her, and she would live.

William Wallace said:

"What thunderclap was that which is able to awaken death or shake the shroud from off a dead man's shoulders?

"Peggy dies?

"If thunder should speak those words, Wallace would swear it lies. Who spoke that, fatal nuncio?"

A nuncio is a messenger.

Old Wallace said:

"His breath who [or Who] gave thee being."

That person, of course, is William Wallace's father. It is also God, who breathed life into Adam.

Old Wallace then said:

"Hazelrigg's returned."

"From where?" William Wallace said. "The devil?"

"From England, and he arrived here this instant," Old Wallace said. "Unless thou come in and surrender thyself, her life dissolves to air."

"May the charitable angels waft her to heaven," William Wallace said.

"Have you decided then to lose her?" Sir John Graham asked.

William Wallace said:

"How shall we save her?

"Singly as I am, I will oppose myself against the town of Lanark, swim the vast moat and, with my trusty sword, hew down the castle gates, unhinge the doors, file off her irons and, through a wall of steel, attempt her rescue!"

"It is impossible!" Old Wallace said.

William Wallace said:

"It is 'impossible.'"

He then asked:

"What's the news from England?"

Old Wallace answered:

"Grimsby, the firebrand of his country, comes to ensnare you. At his heel treads a huge army, led on by the Queen Eleanor, Percy, and Clifford."

Percy and Clifford were English lords and generals.

"Torture, and death itself, cannot divide us," William Wallace said.

Grimsby might be for England now, but he was Scottish. William Wallace believed that he would change sides and support Scotland again.

"Sir John Graham, you shall be the engine our political trickery must work with," William Wallace said. "Immediately spread a rumor that, hearing of the English expedition, our faction has dissolved."

"What's this got to do with Peggy's rescue?" Sir John Graham asked.

William Wallace said:

"Much!

"This rumor once blown throughout the land will stay and delay the English forces and give us time and means to strengthen our forces.

"Once that is done, go to Sir William Hazelrigg, Sir Thomas Selby, and Thorne, emphasize Peggy's innocence and, in return for her freedom and your own, make faith — swear an oath — to yield me to them to be their prisoner.

"The offer will be no doubt accepted. You yourself will be at once pardoned, and your daughter will be free."

"What rests — what remains — for Wallace?" Sir John Graham asked.

William Wallace said:

"Prospered destiny.

"If the great cause we undertake is good

"It will thrive; if not, let it be washed in Wallace's blood."

All exited.

— 1.6. —

Sir William Hazelrigg, Thorne, Sir Thomas Selby, and Sir Jeffrey Wiseacres talked together.

Sir Jeffrey Wiseacres was an English Justice of the Peace.

"Is it by general proclamation voiced — voted — that unless proud Wallace yields, Peg Graham dies?" Sir William Hazelrigg asked.

"The criers are all hoarse from bawling it," Sir Jeffrey Wiseacres said.

Sir William Hazelrigg said:

"It is time for providence to stir. The king (I don't know upon what complaints) pretends and professes that this rank and flourishing rebellion took its root from wrongs in us, rather than from treacheries in Wallace and he sends his forces to examine and question our demeanours rather than their treasons.

"We must prevent — anticipate — it.

"What do you think, Sir Jeffrey?"

"Indeed, I think even as you think," Sir Jeffrey Wiseacres said. "Policy must prevent it."

Policy is politics that involves cunning trickery.

A messenger entered the scene and said, "Sir John Graham craves conference — conversation — with the Commissioners."

Sir William Hazelrigg said:

"Admit him."

Sir John Graham entered the scene.

Sir William Hazelrigg continued:

"A man, I think, of your experience, respect, and education, should not link yourself in such a chain of counterfeits."

The counterfeits were the rebels.

Sir John Graham said:

"Nor have I, Lords. But, for your best advantage and England's good, traitors and dottrels — traitors and dupes — are sold and betrayed for all alike. This is to be done for the general good. He who will take them must seem to do as they do, imitate their vicious actions, strive to take upon him their idle follies, join their company, and drive them into a net without them suspecting a trap."

In other words: Sir John Graham claimed to be pretending to support the rebels so that he could betray them for the good of England.

"So did not Graham?" Sir William Hazelrigg asked.

He was claiming that Sir John Graham had supported and was still supporting the rebels.

Sir John Graham said:

"Speak not before your knowledge."

In other words: Don't speak before you know what you're talking about.

Sir John Graham continued:

"You detain my only daughter as your prisoner.

"Will Selby and his colleagues free her and pardon me if I dissolve the brood of traitors and give up Wallace in bonds?"

Sir Thomas Selby said:

"Let his daughter be produced."

Peggy, guarded, entered the scene.

Sir Thomas Selby continued:

"And let her execution be for a while deferred, although in her cause Selby has lost a son and with him all content and happiness, so dear I tender the peace of Scotland and my sovereign's good that ... give the traitor to the hand of law and with her life, take thine."

His words were ambiguous. They could mean:

1) I will give you Peggy's life if you give me the life of William Wallace. Peggy and you, Sir John Graham, can depart safely, but you, Sir John Graham, will owe me your life.

In this case, Peggy and Sir John Graham would live and William Wallace would die.

2) I will take Peggy's life, and by so doing, I will take the life of you, Sir John Graham. I will do this after receiving William Wallace as my prisoner.

In this case, William Wallace, Peggy, and Sir John Graham would die.

"That is good policy," Sir Jeffrey Wiseacres said.

Peggy said to her father:

"Aye, trow ye mean not Wallace? His *devoire* and doughty valor merits more repute nor such fawe language."

[Aye, I hope you don't mean Wallace? His duty and brave, bold valor merits more and better reputation and no such foul language.]

Devoire is French for "duty." William Wallace is faithful in doing his duty, which is to be loyal to Scotland.

Sir John Graham said:

"He is a foul traitor.

"I have conversed with Wallace, thrown myself into his bosom, mingled thoughts with him, and find him neither worthy of thy love nor of my alliance."

Peggy said:

"Fay! Say not so. My bonny Wallace luifes me."

[Bah! Don't say that. My handsome and admirable Wallace loves me.]

Sir John Graham said:

"Yes, he loves you as a politician loves a knave — for his own ends."

The words "... he loves you as a politician loves a knave — for his own ends" are ambiguous.

Whose own ends? The politicians? Or the knave's? Both?

A love relationship between two people is one that values the ends of both people in the relationship.

Sir John Graham continued:

"Hearing thy death proclaimed unless he came in and surrendered, I told him about it; he smiled.

"I urged and emphasized thy love and constancy; still he smiled."

The reason why "he smiled" may be 1) he was happy that the English had captured Peggy, or 2) he had in mind a trick that could rescue Peggy.

Sir John Graham continued:

"And to confirm it, he basely has cut off all his associates and given himself up wholly to me."

"Basely" can mean "treacherously." But treacherously to whom?

Why would William Wallace wholly give himself up to Sir John Graham? So Sir John can protect him? Or so William Wallace can rescue Peggy?

Peggy said:

"Hawd there, for charity! And wad ye give him to his foes, that gave his blood to your protection?"

[Hold there and stop, for charity! And would you give him to his foes, him who gave his blood — himself — for your protection?]

Did William Wallace give his blood to Sir John Graham so Sir John can protect him? Or has William Wallace previously shed his own blood to protect Sir John Graham?

Of course, William Wallace's foes might give his blood for Sir John Graham's protection: Give us William Wallace, and in return you and your daughter can go away freely.

Sir John Graham said:

"I will, and I have, for thine enlargement — your freedom and benefit — and for my own, I have.

"No more! Here comes the rebel!"

William Wallace, bound and guarded, entered the scene.

He said to Sir John Graham:

"Treacherous man! Is this thy love for me? Are these thy deep promises? Are thou their spy?"

He held up his bound hands and said:

"Look, Selby, here's the hand that cleft thy son's heart in two."

"For which, base villain, I'll see thee hanged," Sir Thomas Selby said.

William Wallace said:

"Thou don't know that. Thine own eyes may feed the crows as soon as mine. Toads and snakes may dig their lodgings in thy breast and devils make faggots — a bundle of sticks — of thy bones first.

"But what is my sentence?"

Sir Thomas Selby said to Sir John Graham, "Here, Graham, for thy service we free thy beauteous daughter."

"A mild exchange," William Wallace said. "Angels approve it."

"Mild" means gentle and kind.

"Next, we restore to thee thy lands and offices," Sir William Hazelrigg said.

An office is a position with certain duties attached. For example, a government job.

Peggy asked, "And what about Wallace?"

"Erase him from your thoughts," Sir Thomas Selby said.

"Erased be his name from the white book of life that speaks it," Peggy said.

In other words: Let anyone who advises me to erase William Wallace from their thoughts have his own name erased from the white book of life: the list of names of those who will enter Heaven.

"Go away from here," Sir Jeffrey Wiseacres said.

Peggy said:

"Dear Wallace, though one shroud

"Hold not our bonds, we shall meet in yonder cloud,"

Using Scottish dialect, Peggy continued:

"Whare no fell Southern now there can extrude,

"Nor bar us fra celestial pulchritude.

"I'd gange thy gait 'til heaven, and as we fly

"Like turtle doves we's bill and find good play."

[Dear Wallace, although one shroud will not hold our two selves, bonded in marriage, we shall meet in yonder cloud — in Heaven — from where no fell Southern man — no deadly Englishman — now can squeeze us out, nor bar us from celestial pulchritude — heavenly beauty and happiness. I'd walk and match thy gait until heaven, and as we fly like turtledoves, we'll kiss and find good play.]

"Match his gait" to heaven sounds as if she will commit suicide when he dies.

The good play could be similar to that found in bed.

Turtledoves are symbols of constancy in love.

In other words: Peggy and William Wallace would not be buried in the same grave, but they would be reunited in Paradise.

Peggy and her father, Sir John Graham, exited.

William Wallace said:

"Rare resolution — splendid determination! What weak heart would faint, having so constant a companion?

"Selby, my soul's bound on a glorious voyage and would be freed out of this jail of flesh. So then do not hinder my voyage."

"Hindering your voyage would not be politically wise," Sir Jeffrey Wiseacres said. "We'll rather set you on your voyage earlier."

Sir William Hazelrigg ordered:

"Raise a gallows fifty foot high."

A person in a noose dropped from that height would be decapitated.

He then said to William Wallace:

"Ye shall not go by water; we'll send you up a nearer way."

In other words: William Wallace would die by hanging, not by drowning.

William Wallace said:

"All's one to me. Any way of dying is fine.

"Axe, halter [noose for hanging], famine, martyrdom, or fire are all just different passages to heaven.

"Let my soul go the furthest way about — let me die slowly.

"Let my soul come tired with — torn by — tortures, shooting out from my heart.

"The deepest wounds, like strong certificates — guarantees of death — will find my kindest welcome."

Carrying a warrant, Grimsby entered the scene and said:

"Stop the execution!

"And, having read this warrant, know that it is the queen's pleasure that you send in this traitor under my conduct and guard to the English camp.

"Rebellion of this nature must be searched and probed with sharper and more painful torture."

"I outdare the worse," William Wallace said. "He who is afraid of death is no man, and Wallace's resolve and determination shall outlive his breath."

Grimsby said:

"It is but short-lived else."

"First see that he is bound and hoodwinked — blindfolded — and then leave him to my care."

"Bear my love with this rebel," Sir Thomas Selby said.

His love and respect were for his sovereign ruler: King Edward I.

"Bear my service, too!" Sir William Hazelrigg said.

He wanted his respects to be paid to Queen Eleanor.

"And bear my policy to the good queen and ladies," Wiseacres said.

"Come, Wallace!" Grimsby said. "Now your pride draws near the fall."

William Wallace said:

"Why, Grimsby, if I fall, it is only to gather stronger force to rise

"For, as a ball's thrown down to raise it higher,

"So death's rebound shall make my soul aspire

"To the glorious clouds. As long as I die secure,

"Death cannot threaten more than I dare endure."

"Die secure" meant "die secure in the belief that his soul would go to Heaven."

The English nobles motioned for guards to go with Grimsby and William Wallace, but Grimsby said, "No, not a man more than my private followers. The queen orders it."

Grimsby and William Wallace exited.

"Farewell, valiant Grimsby, and farewell, Danger," Sir William Hazelrigg said.

William Wallace was a dangerous man.

"Policy and all," Sir Jeffrey Wiseacres said.

Sir Thomas Selby said:

"The traitors having fled and Wallace being thus suppressed,

'My son's blood has been paid and revenged, and his wronged ghost is at rest."

Sir William Hazelrigg said:

"And the whole land is quiet.

"Where's Sir John Graham?"

He had left with his daughter, Peggy.

Sir William Hazelrigg continued:

"We'll make him a partner in commission and delegated authority. It will be a means to make our party strong and keep down mutinies.

"Search out Old Wallace and hang the churl at his own door."

He wanted to hang Old Wallace in front of Old Wallace's house. A signpost could be the place to hang the noose.

Sir William Hazelrigg continued:

"Sir Jeffrey! Place tables in the streets, and provide bonfires and bells."

The tables in the streets, bonfires, and bells were to celebrate William Wallace's capture.

The town was filled with Englishmen.

He continued:

"Since without cause they murmur, let them know that with their knees we'll make their proud hearts bow.

Sir William Hazelrigg believed that the Scots had rebelled without a good reason to rebel.

He continued:

"Sir Jeffrey Wiseacres! Be Master of the Feast. You keep the purse; if money falls out short, send out for more.

"You have commission — the authority — to do that."
Everyone exited.

CHAPTER 2
— 2.1. —

Grimsby, two or three of his followers, and William Wallace, who was bound and hooded, stood together.

"Why do thou talk about conscience?" Grimsby said. "Thou are an apparent and obvious rebel."

"How can he be a rebel who was never a subject?" William Wallace asked. "What right has Edward to the crown of Scotland (the sword except) more than myself, or Grimsby?"

King Edward I's right to rule Scotland lay in his sword: Might makes right.

"What is a greater right than conquest?" Grimsby asked.

When Scotland had a problem with succession, its leaders asked King Edward I to choose the next King of the Scots. King Edward I chose Balliol. He also treated Scotland as a vassal state. Later, the Scots rebelled against England. King Edward I put down the rebellion and forced Balliol into exile.

William Wallace replied:

"What is a juster cause than mine?

"Respected countryman, thou who have been nobly valued and held rank with the best deservers, look upon the wounds and mortal stabs of that distressed breast — Scotland — that gave thee suck.

"See thy poor brethren slaves, thy sisters ravished and raped, and all the outrages that bloody conquest can give licence to.

"See this, and then ask conscience if the man who with his blood seeks general reformation deserves the name of traitor.

"Whither do thou lead me?"

"To Northumberland and Beaumont," Grimsby said.

Percy was the Earl of Northumberland.

"Butchers, do your worst," William Wallace said. "Torture, I spit defiance in thy face. And death, I embrace thee with as kind a name as if thou were —"

He was interrupted by the entrance of Old Wallace, Peggy, Sir John Graham, Friar Gertrid, Comyn, and Menteith.

Old Wallace finished his son's sentence for him, "— thy Father —"

Peggy added, "— and thy waife."

[And thy wife.]

A waif is a stray animal or a homeless person. Probably, the word "wife" is intended, although Peggy is betrothed, not married, to William Wallace.

They released William Wallace and removed the hood that had blinded him.

William Wallace said:

"Am I in heaven or in a slumber? Who can tell me? Speak! Am I dead or living? Or asleep? Or all, or both, or neither? Tell me, Fate!

"I think I see my father, warlike Graham, the friar. What! Peggy, too?

"I ask thee, joy, to not overflow my senses.

"Dearest friends, Peg, father, Comyn, Menteith, Graham!

"See! I am newly molded and here stands the creature who by a warrant granted from the queen formed me from out of a second chaos, breathed new life, new motions, new dimensions into me, so I could tell the story that would shame the world and make all mankind blush."

Sir John Graham and Grimsby had rescued William Wallace from the Englishmen. This would allow William Wallace to tell the story of Scotland's woes and to continue his rebellion against the English.

"My luive!" Peggy said.

[My love!]

Sir John Graham said, "Our prayers —"

Comyn added, "— and all our friendship like a coat of steel stand between him and danger."

William Wallace said:

"All join hands!"

Everyone, including Grimsby, joined hands.

William Wallace continued:

"Thus, like a mountain cedar Wallace stands among a grove of friends, and he will not move from this place for all of Edward's thunder, nor for the frown of Jove.

"I'll hew the yoke from off my country's neck or never house myself — I'll never take shelter.

"This religious friar is a full witness to the sacred bond — the sacred agreement or contract — between heaven and me which, on my part, I'll keep or pay the forfeit with my blood."

Friar Gertrid said:

"Heaven shield! May Heaven defend and protect you!

"Many a tall wood oak will be felled before Wallace stoops."

The tall oaks are important Englishmen.

Friar Gertrid continued:

"Heed Gertrid's saw: my wise saying.

"This sword shall keep in much awe fell — deadly and cruel — Southern folk.

"Many a cry will come from cradled babies, before he shall fly."

The words "he shall fly" are ambiguous. They can mean 1) he shall flee from his enemies, or 2) he (his soul) shall fly to Heaven.

Friar Gertrid continued:

"Nurses' sighs and mothers' tears shall swell the clouds.

"Until thy own blood proves to be false, this crag — your neck — shall never lie dead."

William Wallace said:

"Shall Wallace live until his own blood prove false?

"Why, that can never be, until palsied old age has thrust his icy fingers through my veins and frozen up the passages of blood."

Comyn said, "The town of Lanark, peopled only with English pride and overjoyed with thy surprise — thy ambush and capture — all are made drunk with mirth, bonfires, bells, and banquets, and the devil and all others in the town invite our swords to their sad funeral."

The town of Lanark was filled with Englishmen celebrating the capture of William Wallace. Comyn would like to kill all the Englishmen.

William Wallace said:

"Close — attack — with advantage. Put yourselves in arms and cease their forfeit lives. This holy friar shall first bestow a matrimonial bond on our united love, and then my sword, like winged lightning, shall prepare a way to Lanark's doom."

Friar Gertrid said:

"Nay, by marry, stay awhean!

"Dig not thy whinyard in the weamb of Lanark's town, for if thou gang thou's weark thy life's friend mickle wrang. Thou's come back seafe but, bairn, I fear I'll never blink upon thee mear. Kneel 'til thy sire his benison crave. Next duty is 'til dig his grave.

"Kiss, kiss thy Peg, for well I fear these amorous twins shall ne'er kiss mear 'til in death's arms they kiss. This state stands writ in heaven and sealed by fate."

[No, by the Virgin Mary, stay for a while.

[Don't dig thy sword in the womb of the town of Lanark, for if thou go, thou will work much wrong to thy life's friend. Thou will come back safe, but child, I fear I'll never more see thee. Kneel before thy father and ask his blessing. Thy next duty is to dig his grave.

[Kiss, kiss thy Peg, for well I fear these amorous twins shall never kiss more until in death's arms they kiss. This situation stands written in heaven and is sealed by fate.]

The amorous twins are William Wallace and Peggy — and their lips.

William Wallace said, "Then Fate dissembles with me; this is the second time she has by vision summoned me to arms."

He had not previously mentioned the first time Fate had by vision summoned him to arms.

Everyone exited.

A battle was being fought outside Lanark.

Sir William Hazelrigg met Sir Thomas Selby and Sir Jeffrey Wiseacres.

With Sir Thomas Selby and Sir Jeffrey Wiseacres were Friar Gertrid, Old Wallace, and Peggy.

"Whom have you there?" Sir William Hazelrigg asked.

"We were seeking the cave for shelter," Sir Thomas Selby said. "See whom kind fate has given us."

Sir William Hazelrigg said:

"Treacherous Old Wallace, the doting — foolish — wizard [the friar], and the dissembling woman, chief cause of this rebellion.

"Now Revenge, clothe thee in crimson and prepare to feast.

"We'll tune — play — such dismal music as shall dint smiles in thy shallow cheeks."

The dismal music would dint — put — smiles in the cheeks of personified Revenge.

The personification of Revenge in this case was himself.

Peggy said, "Alas, for woe, what gars this fewde? What ill intend ye, man?"

[Alas, for woe, what causes this bitter hostility? What ill do you intend to do, man?]

"To make Rebellion fatherless and Murder a madding — frenzied — widower," Sir William Hazelrigg said.

To him, the personification of Rebellion and Murder was William Wallace. By killing Old Wallace and Peggy, he could make William Wallace both fatherless and wife-less.

"Oh, spare my old age!" Old Wallace said.

"Pity my beauty!" Peggy said.

"My religion!" Friar Gertrid said.

"Like the pity that thy barbarous son bestowed on my boy's life, I'll print upon thy bosom," Sir Thomas Selby said to Old Wallace.

Sir Thomas Selby stabbed Old Wallace.

Sir William Hazelrigg said, "Thus withered the pride of Lanark, and thus fades the flower that caused their ruin."

Sir William Hazelrigg stabbed Peggy and then exited.

Sir Jeffrey Wiseacres said, "Thus religion's cries were stopped with steel, and thus religion dies."

Sir Jeffrey Wiseacres stabbed Friar Gertrid.

Dying, Old Wallace said, "Wallace! Revenge me as thou are my son."

"Revenge thy wife!" Peggy said.

"Revenge religion!" Friar Gertrid said.

Cries sounded nearby: "Wallace!" and "Conquest!"

Sir William Hazelrigg returned and said:

"May thunderbolts and fire rampier — block like a rampart — your throats!

"The slave William Wallace has grown infinite and moves in every place at once. Shift and look out for yourselves.

"Proud William Wallace, reeking in the blood of Lanark like a fierce tiger nursed in human spoil, pursues the slaughter. The barren hills lie strewn with mangled limbs; such men whom the gentle night rescues from death, fall in the morning flight.

"So then either flee or fall and have the dead for company!

"Flee from a rebel, but may Fate keep true course,

"We'll ebb like floods to flow with stronger force."

According to Sir William Hazelrigg, they would flee for now, but they would soon regroup and become stronger.

Sir William Hazelrigg, Sir Thomas Selby, and Sir Jeffrey Wiseacres exited.

— 2.3. —

The bodies of the dead Friar Gertrid and the dying Peggy and Old Wallace remained behind.

William Wallace, bloody, entered the scene.

He shouted, "Pursue the slaughter, while I —"

Seeing the corpse of Friar Gertrid, he said:

"Salvation shield me!

"Friar Gertrid, answer me! What barbarous hand has cast my friend into this cold dead sweat?

"Tell me, gentle Father. Felon death that has acted sacrilegious burglary and stole my —."

He caught sight of his biological father and his wife and said:

"Father!"

"Wallace?" Old Wallace asked.

"No excuse," William Wallace said, looking at their mortal wounds.

There was no excuse for whoever had murdered his father and his wife.

"Aye, so, husband," Peggy said.

She meant, "Aye, that is true, husband."

William Wallace said:

"Don't entreat me. You are both guilty parties in the dearest robbery."

By dying, they would rob him of their love.

William Wallace continued:

"So then, although you are my wife and father — have mercy, Fate! — don't play the tyrant with me.

"Do not try and test my senses above their weak ability to endure such misery.

"Cease to afflict me, or I shall turn rebel and breathe invectives against thy power."

Peggy said, "O my dear Wallace, for the luive of laife, for luive of awe souls and thy dying waife, list to my latter accents and attend of all thy joys the derne and dismal end."

[O my dear Wallace, for the love of life, for love of old souls and thy dying wife, listen to my last words and learn the dark and dismal end of all thy joys.]

This culture believed that dying people had the gift of prophecy.

"Torture above endurance!" William Wallace said. "King of dreams, dissolve my vision!"

He was hoping that he was dreaming.

"Wallace is awake," Peggy said.

William Wallace said:

"Oh, if I am awake, let my soul never sleep in the blest bosom of my ancestors until I have drawn a sea of purple tears — drops of blood — from forth the bosoms of the murderers.

"Dear Peggy, father, Gertrid. Which way? Where? How? When? What means? What cause shall I devise to find it out and avenge your tragedies?"

Peggy said, "I'll teach ye how. Selby and Hazelrigg be the fell blood-hounds who have hunted laife until these toyles of death."

[I'll teach you how. Selby and Hazelrigg are the cruel and deadly bloodhounds who have hunted life and driven it into these toils — nets and traps — of death.]

"Have they turned hangmen?" William Wallace asked.

Peggy said:

"Religious cries, beauteous entreats, and reverend well-aways could not win Grace or Favor.

"Wallace, revenge my death and for a favor keep my hindmost breath."

[The religious cries of Friar Gertrid, my beauteous entreaties, and the reverend — worthy of respect — laments of your father could not win Grace or Favor from the murderers.

[Wallace, revenge my death and for a remembrance keep my last breath.]

Peggy died.

Seeing some people coming, William Wallace asked, "And who is it here?"

Grimsby, Comyn, Menteith, and Sir John Graham entered the scene.

"Where's Wallace?" Grimsby said. "Never have I seen such a ruthless massacre."

"Grimsby, Wallace can show thee a massacre that will prove that thine is only a May-game," William Wallace said.

May-games are entertainments to celebrate the month of May.

"That would be terrible and strange!" Grimsby said.

William Wallace said:

"Do thou startle at this battle?

"Then see a spectacle strong and forceful enough to stop the motion of the spheres or strike the Sun dead in the brow of heaven."

This culture believed that the Sun, planets, and stars were embedded in concentric, hollow, transparent spheres that revolved around the Earth. The Moon was embedded in one sphere, the Sun was embedded in another sphere, the fixed stars were embedded in a third sphere. The planets (wandering stars) had spheres of their own.

William Wallace continued:

"Look and, like men shot from the bow of thunder,

"Fall senseless; death wounds not as deep as wonder."

Looking at the three corpses of Friar Gertrid, Old Wallace, and Peggy, Grimsby asked, "Whose bloody act was this?"

"These are the bloody acts that were contrived and plotted by experienced villains," William Wallace said.

"Who were the authors of these murders?" Grimsby asked.

William Wallace said:

"Judge. They all spoke English: Death best becomes that dialect.

"The first murder was bloody Hazelrigg's; the second, more villain-like murder was Selby's; but all had a hand in the third murder."

A trumpet sounded.

A messenger entered and announced, "English ambassadors!"

"They are welcome," William Wallace said. "Let not one sullen brow be seen in all this fiery firmament."

He did not want himself or the others to appear to be mourning.

The English ambassadors — Mountford and Glascot — entered the scene. Sebastian, Queen Eleanor's nephew, accompanied him. He was disguised, and he was not an official ambassador.

"Welcome!" William Wallace said. "What is your business here?"

Looking at William Wallace, Sebastian said to himself, "The northern traitor looks far more like a prince than a base rebel."

Mountford said:

"We say this to a rebel from a royal king:

"If Wallace will confess himself a traitor and crave and beg mercy for his bloody outrages and thefts, and submit himself to Edward, there's hope of life."

"The always charitable English," William Wallace said.

He was sarcastic.

Looking at William Wallace, Sebastian said to himself:

"He is not a rebel, to be sure.

"This man does not look like a man who would shake a kingdom."

William Wallace had been speaking quietly and without anger.

Mountford said:

"If he shall deny this offer of peace, then rape, murder, ruin and destruction, and all the sons of war stand striving and competing for the prey and, once they are let loose, they shall not be checked, nor taken up, until rage is tired with murder, and thou thyself in chains are hanged like a villain."

Wallace said:

"This is all perfect English."

To him, English was the dialect of death.

He then asked:

"Have you finished speaking?"

"We have," Mountford said.

William Wallace said:

"Then we will begin to speak.

And this a loyal subject says to a tyrant:

"If Edward will confess himself a tyrant and kingly felon, and make good such theft that he and his have practiced by returning the value of what was stolen, and sue for — appeal for — his peace by yielding up his followers and himself to Wallace, then there's hope of life."

"He and his" are the king and his followers.

William Wallace continued:

"If he shall deny this offer of peace, then rape, murder, ruin, and all the brood of war shall be let fly and never be lured off until they are gorged and bated with the heart of the proud king himself."

Falconers would train a falcon to return with a lure made of feathers and meat.

"To bate" means 1) to come to an end, or 2) to flutter downward. The second meaning applies literally to a falcon.

In other words: If King Edward I does not accept this offer, then war will begin and continue until the heart of King Edward I has been metaphorically eaten.

Sebastian said, "Now speaks a man who would thrust Jove from Olympus."

Jove is Jupiter, king of the gods; he lives on Mount Olympus.

"Calm your anger, for now speaks mercy," Glascot said. "If your country's wrongs grow from abuse in Edward's substitutes, you shall have equal and impartial and fair hearing, and the wrongs will be punished in the deservers."

William Wallace said to himself about the ambassadors' words, "This should not be English or, if it is, King Edward is no tyrant."

"What does Wallace answer?" Glascot asked.

The English ambassadors had made a fair and attractive offer, but they had ignored the corpses of Friar Gertrid, Old Wallace, and Peggy that were in plain sight.

William Wallace said:

"First, please pardon me if, like the working of a troubled sea, my bosom rose in billows, for although the winds that raised the storm are down, yet the dear ruins lie still in view: a father and a wife — age, beauty, and religion."

He said to the corpse of his father:

"For thee thousands shall weep."

He said to the corpse of his wife:

"As many wives shall shed purple tears for thee."

The wives would cry for Peggy, William Wallace's wife, because their husbands had been killed to avenge her death.

He said to the corpse of the friar:

"As many churchmen shall offer their reeking — their steaming — souls in sacrifice."

William Wallace was so angry that he was willing to kill churchmen.

He then said to the English ambassadors:

"Court, city, church, the chamber of your king, the chair of state, shall be no privilege."

The chair of state is the throne.

According to the protocol of war, heralds and ambassadors are not to be harmed. They have safe conduct while they bring messages to and from their king. Cases of spying, however, are an exception.

Looking at the three corpses, Sebastian said, "This was not King Edward's act."

Wallace replied:

"Yet it is the act of such men as Edward placed in commission.

"Oh, it was a churlish storm, and wretched I, like a forlorn survivor, am left to inter their dear remembrances."

Sebastian began, "Good gentlemen —"

William Wallace interrupted, "— but, bid relentless Edward send in the pirates Hazelrigg and Selby and in their hands letters of marque subscribed with his signature to make me master of my own revenge or, like a ball wrapped in a cloud of fire, ruin shall fall upon his palace top, pierce through the roof and, in his chair of state, solicit justice."

Letters of marque gave a person the right to seek revenge upon people from an enemy state. The letters of marque that William Wallace wanted would allow him to kill Sir William Hazelrigg and Sir Thomas Selby.

The fiery ball can be a fiery meteor, aka falling star.

Or the ball may be a cannonball fired from a fiery cannon.

"Into his princely ears, I'll give information about the wrongs done to you," Mountford promised.

"Will Wallace hear my advice?" Grimsby asked.

"Yes," William Wallace answered.

Using the third person to refer to himself, Grimsby said, "Then be ruled by Grimsby. Follow Grimsby's advice."

He whispered in William Wallace's ear.

He had recognized the disguised Sebastian.

William Wallace then said:

"Thanks for thy kindness, Lords Ambassadors.

"We esteem you such. May we crave perusal of your commission?"

"Wallace shall command it," Mountford said.

He showed William Wallace the commission.

William Wallace looked at the commission, and then he said, "Mountford and Glascot are the ambassadors. What third fellow is that?"

He pointed to Sebastian.

"One of our followers," Mountford said.

William Wallace said:

"Good. His name is not inserted in the commission.

"Someone, call out a headsman! Call for an executioner."

Sebastian was not an ambassador and so was not protected by the commission.

"Ambitious rebel!" Sebastian said. "Know that I am a prince and nephew to the queen!"

William Wallace said, "Even if thou were the king, since thou have no part in the official embassy, I'd have thy head."

Wallace pointed to the three men in turn and said to the executioner:

"Go on and strike Sebastian's head off!

"This second man, named Mountford, cut his tongue out.

"This third man, named Glascot, thrust out his eyes.

"And put their followers to the sword: Kill them."

The three Englishmen asked, "Will Wallace be more mild?"

The executioner exited with Mountford, Glascot, Sebastian, and their followers.

William Wallace said:

"Wallace will be more just than see the law of arms disgraced.

"Sound drums and drown their cries!

"Revenge beats at heaven's gates for tyrannies."

The executioner returned with Glascot and Mountford.

Mountford's tongue had been cut off. Glascot had been blinded. Sebastian had been beheaded, and Glascot was carrying Sebastian's head.

Because Sebastian was not an ambassador, he could be regarded as a spy. Because Mountford and Glascot had brought him to the Scottish camp, they could also be regarded as spies.

William Wallace said:

"So now our tragic muse jets — struts — on the stage."

Tragedy is noted for hubris: overweening pride. Often, the protagonist has a tragic flaw.

He said to Glascot, who could speak:

"You, who, because you saw baseness, now lack your sight, bear along with this present — Sebastian's head — our cordial commendations and regards back to the queen, and say that we so much regard her sacred honor, we'd not see it wronged even in her nephew."

Her nephew, Sebastian, had wronged the family honor by being a spy.

He then said to Mountford, who could see:

"You, who, because you spared speech in honor's cause, are now justly mute, conduct this eyeless messenger back to the queen."

Mountford and Glascot had both seen the three corpses but neither had expressed regret about them.

William Wallace then said to Glascot, who could speak:

"Don't abuse our intent in the delivery: Report what happened exactly the way it happened."

He then said to both of them:

"Make speedy haste lest we be there before you.

He then said to Mountford, who could see:

"Share in like — similar — wrong,

"Lend him your eyes, and borrow his tongue."

He then said to Glascot, who could speak:

"If anyone questions you about your harms

"Say that Wallace did it in the right of arms."

The "right of arms" is the cause of military honor.

William Wallace was angry because the three Englishmen had ignored the corpses of his father, his wife, and the friar.

The Englishmen exited.

"This will frighten the English," Grimsby said.

William Wallace said:

"Honored Grimsby, this, and ten thousand thousand more extremes cannot appease my anger.

"You who love and respect me, see that those I love are inhumed — buried.

"I myself, disguised, will be the convoy of the Englishmen to the English camp and I will see how they are treated."

"It will be a dangerous act," Grimsby said.

William Wallace said:

"The fitter man will be him who undertakes it. Wallace would hold himself not worthy of his fate if he would balk at danger.

"Don't try to dissuade me.

"I will go on even if certain death were against my bosom bent;

"There's gain in blood if it's honorably spent."

He exited.

Grimsby said:

"And honorably spent I fear thine blood will be.

"Honored friends, see that those remains of honorable love are cradled in earth; once that is performed, take up arms to avenge their deaths."

The bodies of Old Wallace, Peggy, and Friar Gertrid would be buried.

Grimsby continued:

"Menteith, I await the coming of some special friends, who are by oath bound to assist us.

"Harken — listen — at how their friendly drums chide them for loitering!"

Drums played as soldiers marched.

The Scottish lords Douglas, Macbeth, and Wintersdale entered the scene.

Grimsby said:

"Honored Douglas, welcome!

"Welcome, Macbeth and doughty Wintersdale!

"You could not have brought supply to men more driven in needful want."

They had brought much-needed reinforcements and supplies.

Douglas replied:

"The better are we welcome. Gold to rich men and treasure to the wealthy are known companions.

"Where's our general, the hope-inspiring Wallace?"

Grimsby answered, "He has gone in quest of death, firm as his fate. Because he sees that danger shuns him, he's gone to seek it in the English tents."

"So Hercules sought honor out in hell," Macbeth said. "A man who does not dare to face danger, and who does not dare to out-do the devil, does not deserve the name of general."

One of Hercules' famous labors was to go to the Land of the Dead and remove the three-headed dog Cerberus.

Grimsby said:

"And such a man worthy to be general is Wallace, yet least worth bears him beyond his strength."

William Wallace dares to do much, and he dares to do too much for too little in return.

Grimsby continued:

"Bring up your powers — your armies — for immediate action.

"Wallace's thoughts are tragical and full of blood, active, and violent all."
Douglas said:
"You who best know his thoughts, feed them.
"All that's ours, for Scotland's good, call Wallace's and yours."

53

Wallace had disguised himself as a soldier with wooden legs below the knee and with wooden crutches. As part of his disguise, he spoke with a heavy Scottish accent.

The wooden legs were called stumps.

According to the *Oxford English Dictionary*, one meaning of stump is "A post, a short pillar not supporting anything." The first citation, however, is 1660.

Since William Wallace is not, in fact, legless, this meaning is relevant.

Also according to the *Oxford English Dictionary*, the word "stump" means "A wooden leg." The first citation, however, is 1678.

According to *Dictionaries of the Scots Language*, one meaning of the word "stump" is "The end of a limb from which the hand has been cut." Citations from circa 1420 and circa 1475 are listed.

The disguised William Wallace said to the unable-to-speak Mountford and the blind Glascot, "Whare, man? Till the English camp sent you? God sides! You gang as I ha' seen mony of your countrymen like rank riders amble up westward; you gang the wrang way, man. You shall lose and ye play at shoola-groate; ha' ye na blinkers?"

[Where, man? To the English camp that sent you? By God's sides! You go as I have seen many of your countrymen like rank riders amble up westward; you are going the wrong way, man. You shall lose if you play at shoola-groate; have you no eyes?]

Shoola-groate is a game that is similar to twiddly-winks but uses coins of small value. It can be difficult to control the direction in which the coins are launched, and so the disguised William Wallace meant that Mountford and Glascot were wandering aimlessly.

West of London was Tyburn, where criminals were executed.

Glascot replied, "Alas! I lack my eyes, but I have a tongue; he sees, but he cannot speak."

The disguised William Wallace said, "Blink at smaw faults then. Make me the third man and here's a bonny noise of fiddlers to gang fra winehouse to

winehouse — a blind harper, a mute cornet, and an old Scotch worn to th'
stumps."

[Blink at small faults then. Make me the third man and here's a bonny band
of fiddling musicians to go from winehouse to winehouse — a blind harper, a
mute cornet player, and an old Scotch bagpipe player worn down so much that
he has stumps for legs.]

"Are you a Scotchman, Sir?" Glascot asked.

The disguised William Wallace said:

"Ye, marry am I, body and soul a true Scotchman born, but a true liegeman.
Hang him that does not luife your King and your countryman.

"What gude victuals is that which thilke bonnie man that has glazen
windows to his lindging has tied up in his wallet there?"

[Yes, by the Virgin Mary I am, body and soul a true Scotchman born, but a
true subject to King Edward. Hang him who does not love your King and your
countryman.

[What good food is that which this bonnie man who has glazed windows
to his lodging has tied up in his bag there?]

The glazed windows are blind eyes in his head.

"It is the head of a murdered young gentleman," Glascot said.

The disguised William Wallace said, "What senn you, man? A man's scalp?
I doubt ye be three fawse knaves liggand your heads together about na
goodness: a traitor's head, is't not?"

[What are you saying, man? A man's scalp? I am afraid that you are three
false knaves laying your heads together about no good. It's a traitor's head, isn't
it?]

"No," Glascot said, "but we have met with villains worse than traitors.
William Wallace, your countryman, that bloody hangman, mangled us all three
thus."

The disguised William Wallace said, "Wallace, my countryman? Aye, fay
upon him! So limmer-like, wad I had his head here, too. Iz'd bear it, by my soul,
to the English camp or ne'er gang farder."

[Wallace, my countryman? Aye, damn him! So scoundrel-like. I wish that
I had his head here, too. I'd bear it, I swear by my soul, to the English camp or
never go any further.]

Of course, in an example of dramatic irony, William Wallace's head was present and it was being carried to the English camp.

"His head would be a glorious sight there," Glascot said.

The disguised William Wallace said, "If you could see it, ye should say so, man. Wallace cut off my shanks, too, 'cause I ran away from him to serve your gude prince. Hark, man, I wear na shooen but wodden clampers."

[If you could see it, you would say so, man. Wallace cut off my legs at the knee, too, because I ran away from him to serve your good king. Listen, man, I wear no shoes except wooden clumpers.]

The wooden shoes were wooden legs, which made him walk clumsily: clump, clump, clump.

Of course, William Wallace still had his legs, so these clampers / clumpers were fake wooden legs: veneers that fit over his shins if these parts of his body could be seen. Possibly, he was also wearing wooden clogs as part of his disguise.

"Out of charity, lead us to the English camp," Glascot requested. "You shall, besides receiving our thanks, be most royally paid."

The disguised William Wallace said, "Gang alang, man, 'tis hard by now. A man's head? I deemp'd the poor man had gangand long to law and so was thrust out of doors by head and shoulders."

[Keep going, man. The English camp is nearby now. A man's head? I suspect that the poor man had gone a long time to law and so was violently thrust out of doors by his head and shoulders.]

In a way, Sebastian had gone long to law. He had believed that he was supporting his king and queen.

Another kind of going long to law is engaging in many lawsuits over a long time. Lawyers go long to law.

Some lawsuits result in much misery.

"No law was ever as cruel as Wallace is," Glascot said.

The disguised William Wallace said, "Nay, marry? No law so cruel? Fay, man, fay! I looked upon a man of law not lang since, that sent an awde man and his wife and many bairns a-begging. He had better slizand their weazoned pipes and cut their heads off. But whay was he so bludy-minded, think ye?"

[No, by the Virgin Mary? No law so cruel? Bah, man, bah! I looked upon a man of law not long ago, who sent an old man and his wife and many children begging. He would have done better and been more merciful if he had slit their windpipes and cut their heads off. But why was he so bloody-minded, do you think?]

"I cannot judge," Glascot said.

The disguised William Wallace said, "Marry, man, to get possession of the poor man's house; but there was a cat ganged beyond the man a law."

[By the Virgin Mary, man, to get possession of the poor man's house; but there was a cat that went beyond the comprehension of the man of law."

The cat had outsmarted the lawyer.

"A cat goes beyond a lawyer?" Glascot said. "How?"

The disguised William Wallace said:

"I'll tell you how. The man of law being got in, the cat outreach'd him and leaped to th' top of the lindging and standand on the tiles; the man of law, scorning any one to be abuise him, offers to fling and dingand down the poor pusscat, but she miaowed at him and cried, 'Hawd, thou foul loon, hawd. As thou thrusts out this poor man and his bairns, so there is ane abuife shall thrust out thee.'

"Stay, blind man, here comes soldiers!

[I'll tell you how. The lawyer being got in possession of the house, the cat outreached him and leaped to the top of the lodging and stood on the roof tiles. The lawyer, scorning any one to abuse him, attempted to fling something and knock down the poor pussycat, but she meowed at him and cried, "Halt, thou foul loon, halt. As thou thrust out this poor man and his children, so there is One above Who shall thrust out thee."

[Wait, blind man, here come soldiers!]

Of course, the cat was making the point that God would punish the lawyer for his evil deed.

Bolt, who was Sir Jeffrey Wiseacre's clerk, entered the scene with three or four tattered English soldiers.

The soldiers said, "Stand! *Qui va là*? Spies about our trenches!"

Qui va là is French for "Who are you?" Many English soldiers were serving or had served in France.

Bolt said:

"And see, they have knocked some man down."

He may have been referring to the disguised William Wallace, who was using wooden crutches.

Bolt then asked:

"Sirrah! You who carry two faces under a hood, who are you?"

A two-faced person is a hypocrite, but Bolt may have been referring to Glascot because he was carrying Sebastian's head.

"He must be pressed," the first soldier said. "He will not speak."

The word "press" can mean 1) strongly encouraged, 2) impressed — drafted — to be a soldier, or 3) tortured by having heavy weights placed on a person's chest. Some people who refused to confess were pressed to death.

"Who are thou?" Bolt said. "I order thee to tell me! Have thou a tongue in thy head? Give the word!"

"He has no tongue indeed, sir," Glascot said.

Bolt said:

"He has two heads and not one tongue.

"Who are you who like a blind ass stand still and cannot tell us so?"

"I'm blind indeed," Glascot said. "Conduct us to the lords in the English camp."

"What! Lords?" the second soldier said. "Are you ladies and so you long for lords?"

Bolt said:

"Do you take us for fools? You want us to go tell the lords that here's a dumb man who would speak with them?"

"Dumb" means "unable to speak."

Bolt then asked the disguised William Wallace:

"Who are you, sirrah? Come, halt not! Let's not find you in two tales. That would be best for you."

The word "halt" means 1) limp, and 2) hesitate.

A liar might hesitate while thinking about which lie would be best to tell.

People who tell "two tales" are liars.

The disguised William Wallace said: "I'z a Scotsman, sir! Ye shall ne'er find me in twa tales."

[I'm a Scotsman, sir! You shall never find me in two tales — I'm not a liar.]

Bolt said, "A Scotsman, sir? Do you know where you are, sir, with your blue bonnet on before an English scull? Where's your leg, sir, when an officer speaks to you?"

Scotsmen wore blue hats, and English soldiers wore an armored scull: an armored skullcap.

In this society, "to make a leg" means "to bow." And in this society, one meaning of "leg" is "bow."

The disguised William Wallace said, "My leg, sir, is not in my galligaskin and slop, as yours is. I'z a pure Scotch soldier out at heels and am glad to bestir my stumps. Guide these gude men, your wronged countrymen wha that fawse traitor Wallace has misusand in sike wise."

[My leg, sir, is not in my clothing [breeches and tunic], as yours is. I'm a pure Scotch soldier out at heels and am glad to bestir my stumps. Guide these good men, your wronged countrymen whom that false traitor Wallace has mistreated in such a way.]

"Out at heels" means "impoverished" or "in difficult circumstances." Literally, it means that one's stockings have worn out at the heel.

"Wallace!" the soldiers said. "Oh, the slave!"

Bolt said, "Fellows in arms out at elbows, I shall live to give fire to my piece — firearm — with a burnt inch of match made of that rascal's stomach fat."

"Out at elbows" means "impoverished" or "in difficult circumstances." Literally, it means that one's shirts and coats have worn out at the elbows.

The disguised William Wallace said, "By my soul, sir, wad I might come to th' making of sike a match?"

[By my soul, sir, I wish that I might come to the making of such a match.]

"Here's my hand," Bolt said. "Because thou say so, thou shall be nearby when I make him give fire to my touch-hole."

The touch-hole was part of a weapon such as a cannon. Fire was touched to a hole, lighting gunpowder, and the cannon shot a cannonball.

A touch-hole can also be a vagina or an anus. "Fire" can be sexual fire.

Queen Eleanor, Clifford, Percy, Beaumont, and others entered the scene.

Clifford, Percy, and Beaumont were English lords.

The disguised William Wallace said to himself, "The lords are going to view the trenches."

Bolt said:

"Every man to his parapet! To your trenches, you tattered rogues!"

Parapets are defensive banks of earth raised in front of a trench.

Probably, the soldiers should have already been at their stations. Thus, Bolt's quick order for them to go to their trenches.

"It's well done, fellows!" Clifford said, sarcastically.

Bolt said:

"I beg your Lordship's mercy, but this blind buzzard here cannot see."

He asked Glascot:

"To where will you march headlong, my friend?"

"What men are these?" Percy asked, pointing to the disguised William Wallace and Glascot and Mountford.

"I leave them to your honors' sifting and interrogation," Bolt said. "I have fortifications to look after."

"There's some drinking money for you," Clifford said, giving him a tip. "Go to your works."

"Bless your honors!" Bolt said.

Bolt and his soldiers exited.

"What men are these, I ask?" Percy said. "Will no man speak?"

Glascot said:

"Here and in hearing, with the sound unheard, is youthful Sebastian, nephew to the queen.

"He, longing to see the man famed for the excess of goodness and of badness, although he was not an official part of the honored embassy, disguised himself and risked being in the rebel Wallace's presence."

"Glascot and Mountford!" Percy said, realizing who they were.

"Who did this damned villainy?" Clifford asked.

Glascot said, "Once our message was told to the traitor, who was newly set on fire with madness, showing us the mangled bodies of a friar, his wife, and his father, he burst out into flames high, hot, and violent, in fierce rage. The rebel Grimsby recognized Sebastian (although herald-like he went in disguise) and William Wallace seized him and us for three intelligence-gathering spies. He then cut off Sebastian's head, Mountford's tongue, and Glascot's eyes."

Percy said, "Hang this man. Provide for these men. Truss him up!"

He wanted the disguised William Wallace, who was dressed like a Scot, to be hung, and he wanted Mountford and Glascot to be taken care of.

He had not recognized William Wallace; he simply wanted every Scot to be hung.

The disguised William Wallace said, "What sen ye, man?"

[What are you saying, man?]

Mountford and Glascot exited.

Percy said, "What slave, what Turk, who murders his own brethren dares to play the tyrant thus? Hang all the nation whom we have taken to mercy. I'll not spare fathers, nor mothers, nor their bawling children. Set fire to their houses! Hang up this tyke first."

A "tyke" is a churl.

Turks had a reputation for cruelty. Some Turks murdered their brothers so they could seize the crown.

The disguised William Wallace said:

"Ah, bonnie men, I met 'em playand at bo-peep, and gangand out of their way, and shall I be hanged for my good deeds of charity?

"I'z a poor Scotch soldier, and am run away from that rebel Wallace to feightand for your good prince. Ah, he's a gude king, and y'are all bonnie men. I'zll follow ye all to the death, and to the devil, and ony man dare gang so far.

"For all my crutches, if I clutch Wallace he'll ne'er carry it 'till hell nor heaven."

Bo-peep lost her sheep in the nursery rhyme, and Mountford and Glascot had lost their way.

[Ah, handsome men, I met them playing at bo-peep, and going in the wrong direction and out of their way, and shall I be hanged for my good deeds of charity?

[I'm a poor Scotch soldier, and I have run away from that rebel Wallace to fight for your good prince. Ah, he's a good king, and you are all handsome men. I'll follow you all to the death, and to the devil, if any man dare go so far.]

His final sentence was ambiguous: "For all my crutches, if I clutch Wallace he'll ne'er carry it 'till hell nor heaven."

"Carry it" means "win, achieve a victory."

The Englishmen understood him to be saying:

[For all my crutches, if I clutch Wallace, he'll never be victorious until he dies and wins hell and not heaven.]

But in Scottish dialect, "till" means "to."

Wallace, therefore, meant:

[For all my crutches, if I clutch Wallace, he'll never be victorious to hell and not heaven.]

In other words: William Wallace's victories will be for heaven and not for hell. Heaven will regard Wallace's victories as good.

Percy said, "If he does win victories, may Percy's name be crossed out of the roll of men."

The roll of men is a list of still-living soldiers. Or it may be a list of men who are worthy of being called men.

Clifford said, "So much swears Clifford."

His words were ambiguous, but he was talking about Percy's name — not his own — being crossed out of the roll of men.

Percy said to the disguised William Wallace, "Don't sneak away, sirrah! You are not gone yet. We aren't done with you."

The disguised William Wallace said, "I ken it very weel. I'z not gangan to hanging yet."

[I know it very well. I'm not going to the place of hanging yet.]

Clifford said:

"Yet, although he is a traitor, let me speak thus much for the absent William Wallace.

"Imagine that his situation were your own (or the situation of one who is baser — less well born — but who has spirit).

"A murdered father and a bleeding wife mangled before him would strike fire in snow, make loyalty turn traitor, and make obedience forget all duty."

In other words: If you or any other spirited man had experienced what William Wallace had, you would have experienced emotions that would make you turn traitor.

Queen Eleanor said, "But what about our nephew's death and the disgrace done to our ambassadors?"

Clifford said, "Ambassadors then put off their title, and put on the name of spies when, in their companies, they take disguised observers."

In other words: When the ambassadors took the disguised non-ambassador Sebastian with them, they ceased to be ambassadors and became spies.

Spies can be executed in times of war.

The disguised William Wallace said to himself, "By my soul, the English are gallant men."

Percy, the Earl of Northumberland, asked, "Is there no snare to entrap this wolf?"

Clifford said:

"What, Northumberland, entrap a foe? Surely, 'entrap' is no English word. Clifford, at least, was never acquainted with it.

"Give him fair summons, dare him to come to the battlefield, and trap him then."

In other words: Fight fairly. Call him to the battlefield, fight a battle with his men, and capture him fairly during the battle.

"Ah, bonnie good man!" the disguised William Wallace said to himself.

"His being a traitor warrants and allows deception," Percy said. "Dispatch a second message with acknowledgement of former wrongs to our ambassadors, with promise of a friendly interview early tomorrow, impartially to hear their wrongs, and mildly minister redress."

This is ambiguous. Were the former wrongs done to the ambassadors: the maimings of Mountford and Glascot? Or were they done by the English to the Scots? Was one of the wrongs bringing Sebastian with them? Are the ambassadors mentioned new ambassadors who will carry the message?

Clifford said: "Ensnare him so and don't spare the evildoers, for you'll find, I fear, that Selby, Hazelrigg, and the rest lay yokes too heavy on the nation's neck."

In other words: Selby, Hazelrigg, and the rest have treated the Scots so badly that the Scots are justified in rebelling.

"If they in fact lay yokes too heavy on the nation's neck, punish them," Queen Eleanor said.

"Punish them?" Clifford said. "By God's death, hang them!"

Percy asked, "Shall we agree to have such a message — a lying message — sent that would lure this bloody tiger into the net and, waking then or sleeping, kill him?"

"No!" Clifford said.

"All stratagems are lawful against a foe," Percy said.

"Do what you will, but you will not receive my consent," Clifford said.

"I'll venture to go to the rebel," Beaumont said.

He was a brave man, but he wanted to carry a lying message to William Wallace.

Percy said:

"Do, good Beaumont."

He then asked the disguised William Wallace:

"Scotchman, do thou dare to conduct him as his guide?"

Clifford said, "But be sure to return to us, sirrah, or the next time we take ye, your crag — your neck — shall pay for it."

The disguised William Wallace said:

"Iz'll not run away fra' ye. If I do, hang me and draw me.

"Come, bully Jo; I dare not gang to the Scottish camp, they'll so fly upon me, I'll ne'er come back again; but Iz'll bring you where ye shall see that loon Wallace."

[I'll not run away from you. If I do, hang me and draw me.

[Come, good fellow. I dare not go to the Scottish camp because they'll so fly upon me that I'll never come back again, but I'll bring you where you shall see that loon Wallace.]

Being hung and drawn is a horrible punishment. First the person was dragged on a hurdle to the place of execution, hung by his neck for a while, and then while he was still alive, his intestines were drawn out of his body and burned.

"That's all I wish," Beaumont said. "Lead on!"

The disguised William Wallace said, "Marry, sall I. Luke to yourself, I'll thrust you into the dewle's chops."

[By the Virgin Mary, I shall. Look after yourself. I'll thrust you into the devil's jaws.]

Beaumont said, "As for getting out of the devil's jaws, let me scuffle on my own."

Beaumont and the disguised William Wallace exited.

Queen Eleanor said, "Let's consult for — have a conversation about — actions to be carried out immediately!"

The others consulted with Queen Eleanor while Clifford stayed apart from them and said to himself:

"What is, what should, what can this Wallace be whom fame limns out for — that is, portrays as — such a gallant piece, and is so careful in her workmanship that no part of him deforms him?

"Yet Wallace is a rebel; his chief shame is poverty of gentry."

William Wallace was not highly born, although he became a Scottish knight (a member of the lesser nobility) a few months after the Battle of Stirling Bridge. One way of getting a higher social rank was to win it in battle or in other service to one's country. Many soldiers became knights because of their performance on the battlefield.

Clifford continued saying to himself:

"By my sword, if it would be no reproach to my dear ancestors, I well could spare him some of my unused titles.

"Or I wish that we were at martial gaming, so I might lose and Wallace win so much of Clifford's honor that our stocks might be alike."

"Martial gaming" is a battle.

Clifford continued:

"But I go too far.

"This night he shall be betrayed."

He thought a moment, and then he said to himself:

"No, he shall not be betrayed. I'll turn traitor first, but he shall not be betrayed."

Seeing Clifford apart from the others, Percy came over to him.

Clifford said quietly but strongly:

"Call Beaumont back or else, by Clifford's honor — this is an oath that I esteem more than my life — I will turn traitor and reveal your plots."

Traitors could receive a death sentence.

Clifford continued:

"Call him back!"

"Is Clifford mad?" Percy asked.

"No!" Clifford said. "Percy's lunatic. Suppose that he is a traitor and suppose that the discipline of the field allows the act of entrapment, what honor is it for a herd of yours to torment a sleeping bear? Go and call him back!"

What honor is there is there in lying to and entrapping a man?

Beaumont returned, carrying a wooden leg: one of the ones that William Wallace had used in his disguise.

"Look!" Percy said. "He comes back without being called back!"

"What is the news?" Clifford asked.

"News, do you call it?" Beaumont said. "Let no Scot come near your tents. Wallace sends you this token."

"Huh!" Clifford said. "Who? Wallace?"

"Was that Scot with the crutches the traitor Wallace?" Percy asked.

"By Mars' helmet, he is a complete warrior!" Clifford said. "I so love his worth that I'll court it with my sword."

He respected Wallace so much that he would deliberately seek him out in battle so that he could fight him.

Beaumont said:

"If you had just stood within distance of this thunder (for we parted just where our trenches ended), you'd have sworn the God of War had spoken!

"He said, 'Tell Percy that he shall not need to hunt me in my tent because I'll rouse him in his own tent,' and he told me to give you, Percy, this wooden stump and swears to make you wear it if you dare to fight him in the battlefield."

Game animals are roused from their sleeping places by being made so frightened that they run away from them.

"Base rebel!" Percy said. "Why doesn't he dare to stand and fight here?"

Clifford said:

"None prayed him — asked him to — stay.

"It was manners, being not welcomed, to get away."

In other words: No one asked him to stay here. Since he was not wanted here, it was good manners for him to go away.

Beaumont said:

"He sends his compliments to Clifford, with this wish:

"'That if, at this great match of life and death, Wallace should happen to lose the smallest part of his military honor, then he hopes that Clifford's sword may win it. Clifford knows best how to use his sword."

Clifford could win the honor that Wallace loses by defeating and capturing or killing Wallace honorably in battle.

Beaumont continued:

"'At my return from France,' said Wallace, 'this vow that I have promised shall be surely paid.

"'Our country, overtopped with tyranny, makes us fly to France for succour.

"'Aeolus, god of the winds, let favorable winds and tides assist me.'

"That spoken, the rebel Grimsby and his soldiers met him bearing arms: weapons. What actions further he intends, listen to what their drum tells.

"Here my commission ends."

Clifford said, "Let's send him commendations, too. Beat our drums, too!"

CHAPTER 3
— 3.1 —

Sir Jeffrey Wiseacres and Bolt talked together on a seashore in English-occupied Scotland. Bolt was carrying a trunk that had washed up on shore following a storm.

Bolt, a comic character, was Wiseacres' clerk.

"Set it down, Bolt," Sir Jeffrey Wiseacres said. "I can bear with thee no longer."

Bolt put the trunk down and said:

"No more can I bear any longer with you, Sir Jeffrey."

Bolt was punning on "bear": 1) carry, and 2) endure, put up with.

He continued:

"But what a reeling drunken sot is this sea that casts up such gobbets — lumps of food — as this.

"Is this a windfall or no? Now, Sir Jeffrey, your worship knows both the tags and point of the law."

Windfalls are 1) something that falls (e.g., an apple) because it is blown down by wind, and 2) an unexpected acquisition.

Points are laces, and tags are the metal ends of laces. Bolt meant that Sir Jeffrey knew the finer points of law and knew its ends (purposes). Some legal contracts can be used to metaphorically "tie up" people.

"Yes, to be sure it is a windfall," Sir Jeffrey Wiseacres said. "For, as we walked upon the shore, we saw the ship split, and this trunk fell out. The winds were the cause, so therefore it must necessarily be a windfall."

The trunk had floated to shore after the shipwreck.

"Well, somebody has had but a bad fish dinner today," Bolt said.

That somebody was the dinner for fish.

"The seas have crossed them that sought to cross the seas, and therefore, for my part, I'll never meddle with these water works," Sir Jeffrey Wiseacres said.

"Cross" means 1) opposed and thwarted, and 2) travel across.

"Nor I," Bolt said. "Let's be wiser than a number of gallants and keep the land that's left us."

The court lifestyle was expensive, and some gallants sold land they had inherited to keep up with the other court gallants.

Bolt continued:

"Did you ever see such gambols as the waves made, Sir Jeffrey?"

"Never since I wore the nightcap of justice and never since this here dudgeon dagger was at my side," Sir Jeffrey Wisesacres said.

The nightcap of justices is a blackcap that a justice wore when pronouncing the death sentence. The justice's dagger had a hilt made of the wood called dudgeon.

A hanging man can dance — gambol — on air before he dies.

"Did you note what puffing the winds made until they got great bellies, and then how sorely the ship fell in labor?" Bolt asked.

"Great bellies" are 1) full sails, and 2) pregnant bellies.

Bolt was also punning on "labor."

"Did you hear what a doleful cry they made when their main-yard was split?" Sir Jeffrey Wiseacres asked.

The main-yard is a spar from which hangs the main-sail.

Bolt answered, "Alas, Sir, wouldn't it make any man roar who had but an inch of feeling or compassions in his belly, to have his main-yard split."

This particular main-yard may be a penis.

Bolt continued:

"And how the mariners hung by the ropes like Saint Thomas Onions."

Saint Thomas Aquinas was a fat man: He was round like an onion.

Onions for sale were sometimes displayed on ropes in markets.

"I saw it, Bolt, with salt eyes," Sir Jeffrey Wiseacres said.

His tears were salty.

"So that you may see at sea," Bolt said. "However the wind blows, if a man be well hung, he's cock sure."

"Well hung" refers to sails, but it also means what you think it means.

"Cock sure" means 1) confident, and 2) knows he has a penis that can reliably rise to the occasion.

Sir Jeffrey Wiseacres pointed to the chest and said, "But Bolt, what do thou think this is filled with?"

"A matter of some weight, as I take it," Bolt said.

"Some weight" means 1) heavy weight, and 2) of importance.

"I hope it is gold, it is so heavy, and it was going out of the land," Sir Jeffrey Wiseacres said.

"Going out of the land" may mean "going from one country across the sea to another."

Bolt said:

"Likely enough, for gold goes now very heavily from us, and silver, too. Both red chinks and white chinks fly away."

Red chinks are gold coins, while white chinks are silver coins.

Chinks clink when they hit each other.

Bolt continued:

"But, Sir Jeffrey, if this is gold, how rich is the sea, do you think, that has innumerable such sands?"

One meaning of "sand," as defined by the *Oxford English Dictionary*, is this: "The action of sending; that which is sent, a message, present; (God's) dispensation or ordinance."

The trunk is something sent. The trunk was being sent from one place to another.

Sir Jeffrey Wiseacres could very well regard the trunk as a gift from God, especially if it contained gold.

The ocean has many sands, both on its shores and in shipwrecks containing treasure.

"More rich than the land, and more fat," Sir Jeffrey Wiseacres said.

"More fat" means richer and more fertile.

"So it had need, for the land looks hungry with a lean pair of cheeks," Bolt said, "yet it has an excellent stomach, for it digests anything."

According to the *Oxford English Dictionary*, a figurative meaning of "cheek" is "The outer part of an arm or inlet of the sea."

Sir Jeffrey Wiseacres said, "Then it is like the sea, for all is fish that comes to net there."

"I'll tell you the mystery of that," Bolt said. "Look what mouths gape at land; the same gape at sea. All the land is one kingdom, and all the sea another."

"To gape" is to open the mouth wide. People can do that literally out of hunger or metaphorically out of greed.

The rich often take advantage of the poor.

"And people in it," Sir Jeffrey Wiseacres said.

Bolt said, "And people in it (right worshipful), but they all go westward."

West of London was Tyburn, where criminals were executed.

Bolt continued:

"As there are good and bad here, so there are good and bad there; fools are here, fools are there. As great men here eat up the little men, so whales feed upon the lesser fishes."

"Perhaps then, the watery commonwealth are ill governed?" Sir Jeffrey Wiseacres asked.

"No, they are bravely — splendidly — governed. For heroical Hector Herring is the king of fishes."

Hector was the greatest Trojan warrior in the Trojan War. His name connotes the highest nobility and valor.

"So?" Sir Jeffrey Wiseacres asked.

"Rich cobs are his good subjects who, at the fishing port of Yarmouth, lay down their lives in his quarrel," Bolt said. "Swordfish and pike are his guard."

"Cobs" are the heads of red herring. "Red" is commonly used in literature of the Elizabethan, Jacobean, and Carolinian ages to describe the color of gold, and gold is associated with rich men.

Swords and pikes are weapons. Pikes have pointed heads at the end of a long wooden shaft. It is a thrusting spear.

"Go on," Sir Jeffrey Wiseacres said.

Bolt said:

"Fresh cods are the gallants, and sweet flipper are the knights, whiting-mops are the ladies, and lily-white mussels are the waiting gentlewomen."

Gallants were well-dressed and used perfume, and so they were fresh.

Cods are scrotums, and many gallants chased women.

Some sea animals have flippers.

One meaning of "flip" is blow, and knights give blows in battles.

This society prized light skin more than dark skin.

"Dangerous meat, to take too much of," Sir Jeffrey Wiseacres said.

"But who are the pages?" Bolt asked.

"Shrimps," Sir Jeffrey Wiseacres said.

Pages are boy-servants, and so they are short.

Bolt objected, "No, no, Sir! Periwinkles are the pages, periwinkles."

Periwinkles are a type of mollusc. Proverbially, they are something of little value.

According to *Dictionaries of the Scots Language*, proverbially and allusively, wilks are "The type of something of little value, trivial or amoral."

The prefix peri- means "all around."

The suffix -le means "continuous action."

According to Bolt, pages are continually useless in everything.

"Are there no justices among the fish?" Sir Jeffrey Wiseacres asked.

"Yes, Sir Jeffrey," Bolt replied. "Thornbacks are the justices, and crabs are the constables whom, if you butter them with good words, it is passing midnight!"

Thornbacks had sharp thorns along their backs. Justices can be sharply censorious.

Butter up the crabby constables with praise, and they will let you go past them after midnight, despite curfews.

Sir Jeffrey Wiseacres laughed.

Bolt said, "Dogfish are jailors, and stockfish are the poor common people."

In this society, being called a dogfish was an insult.

Stockfish are dried fish. Before stockfish was cooked, it was beaten to tenderize it. The word "stockfish" was also used as a contemptuous form of address.

"Indeed they live hardly — with difficulty," Sir Jeffrey Wiseacres said.

"But Sir, they are beaten to it," Bolt said. "Then you have wet eels for whores, and great oysters for bawds."

One meaning of "eel" is penis.

"Why great oysters for bawds?" Sir Jeffrey asked.

"Because, for the most part, they are stewed," Bolt said.

The stews are brothels. Stewed prunes were regarded as aphrodisiacs, and they were widely available in brothels.

As a verb, "to stew" can also mean "to stink."

"Very good!" Sir Jeffrey Wiseacres said.

Bolt said, "Lastly, because no kingdom can stand without laws, and because lawyers and pettifoggers swarm to where law has her eyes, the lawyers here therefore are sharks, and gudgeons are the poor clients."

Justice is blind, and so pettifoggers go where law has eyes.

According to the *Oxford English Dictionary*, a pettifogger is "a lawyer who engages in petty quibbling and cavilling, or who employs dubious or underhanded legal practices; a lawyer who abuses the law. Usually derogatory."

Gudgeons are small fish that are used for bait.

William Wallace called from a distance, "Wa! Ho, ro! Sol, fa! Sol, fa!"

These syllables are used by falconers to call to their falcons.

Bolt said, "Hark! Listen!"

"Peace, Bolt!" Sir Jeffrey Wiseacres said. "Be quiet, Bolt!"

He had a trunk that he wished to keep. The person calling might be its owner.

Bolt replied, "Nay, peace you, good Sir Jeffrey! You be at peace! Peace, Peace!"

William Wallace called, "Sol, la! Sol, la! Sol, la! Sol, la!"

Bolt said:

"Some falconer is teaching his hawk pricksong."

Pricked-up ears are listening ears, and a falconer teaches a hawk to listen to him.

"Pricksong" is also melody performed in counterpoint.

Bolt then asked:

"Shall I mock him in his own key?"

"Do," Sir Jeffrey Wiseacres said.

"Sol, fa! Sol, fa! Here, boy!" Bolt called.

William Wallace, who was wet with seawater, entered the scene, calling:

"Here, boy! Wa, ha! Ho, ho!"

Seeing Bolt and Sir Jeffrey Wiseacres, he said:

"All hail to you two."

"And all snow to you, Sir," Bolt said.

"Hail" can mean 1) greetings (Wallace), or 2) ice crystals that fall from the sky (Bolt).

"Sirrah!" Sir Jeffrey Wiseacres said. "Who are thou who wishes all the hail to fall upon us two?"

Bolt said, "Answer wisely to my master, for he's a Justice of Peace, and you'll be smelt out."

Smelt are young salmon. "To be smelled out" means "to be detected."

"I am a drowned rat," William Wallace said.

"A rat?" Sir Jeffrey Wiseacres said.

"Do you take Sir Jeffrey for a rat-catcher?" Bolt said. "You'll tell a sweet tale for yourself soon."

The Pied Piper of Hamelin is a famous fairy tale about a rat-catcher.

"May the pox rot you!" William Wallace said. "I am shipwrecked. Give me some food."

"Shall I make his mittimus?" Bolt asked Sir Jeffrey Wiseacres. "He begs, sir."

Begging without a license was against the law. A mittimus is a warrant to arrest beggars who are unlawfully begging.

"I have met more than my match," William Wallace said. "Neptune and I, wrestling for falls, he got the mastery. I'm bruised, weary, cold, and weak with his beating, and I am liquored soundly."

He was thoroughly wet and had swallowed sea water.

William Wallace had metaphorically wrestled with Neptune, god of the sea, and had been bested. Although Wallace said that he had lost the wrestling match, he still had made it to shore and did not drown.

"He's drunk," Bolt said.

"Yet I am so thirsty that I scarcely can speak," William Wallace said. "If you are men, help me to food and fire."

The salty sea water he had swallowed made him thirsty. He was also hungry and cold.

"What countryman are thou, sirrah?" Sir Jeffrey Wiseacres asked.

"A Scot," William Wallace said. "Give me some victuals, please."

Victuals are food.

"No mind but of thy belly," Bolt said.

"Sirrah, sirrah, you are a Scot, and I am a true English Justice of the Peace," Sir Jeffrey Wiseacres said.

"Not a word of Latin, neither Justice nor Clerk," Bolt said.

Neither he nor Sir Jeffrey knew Latin, although they should know it because of their positions as Justice and Clerk.

Sir Jeffrey Wiseacres said:

"Peace, Bolt! In the king's name, I charge thee to be quiet about that."

He then said to William Wallace:

"If thou will eat bread, earn bread.

"Take up this luggage, sirrah; follow me home to my house, and thou shall have good bread, good drink, and good fire.

"Up, I command thee!"

"I am necessity's slave, and now I must bear," William Wallace said.

He was forced to bear both the trunk and Sir Jeffrey's words.

"Must?" Bolt said. "Nay, shall! Are not the English your good lords and masters?"

"Well, they are," William Wallace said.

He did not say what they are.

"Do you grumble, sir, about Sir Jeffrey?" Bolt asked.

Sir Jeffrey Wiseacres said:

"Keep an eye on him, Bolt, lest he give us the slip."

He then asked William Wallace:

"And were you in this terrible storm at sea, do you say?"

"Over head and ears, sir," William Wallace said.

He was completely underwater at times.

Bolt said:

"If the execution had been upon the land, Sir Jeffrey, as it was upon the sea, your worship would have been in a worse pickle than he."

The execution of the mittimus was a failure as Wiseacres had not gotten and served one.

William Wallace had failed in the wrestling match with Neptune and had been completely underwater.

If Sir Jeffrey Wiseacres' failure was analogous to Wallace's failure, then Wiseacres ought to be completely under land: in his grave.

"Why, knave? Why?" Sir Jeffrey Wiseacres asked.

"Because he who has a bad name is half-hanged, and your worship knows that you have only an ill name," Bolt said.

A bad name is a bad reputation.

The name "Wiseacres" is made of two words: "wise" and "acres."

"Thou varlet!" Sir Jeffrey Wiseacres said. "Is not 'wise' good?"

"Yes," Bolt said.

He said to William Wallace, "Come along, porter!"

Bolt then said:

"'Wise' is good."

"And is not 'acre' good?" Sir Jeffrey Wiseacres said.

"Acres" are land, and ownership of land is good.

"Yes, surpassingly good," Bolt said.

"Why should Wiseacres, being those two words put together, be nought then?" Sir Jeffrey Wiseacres said.

"Nought" is nothing, and it glances at "naughty."

"Isn't plum-porridge good, Sir Jeffrey?" Bolt asked.

"Yes," Sir Jeffrey Wiseacres answered.

The hungry William Wallace said, "I wish that I had this trunk full of them."

By "them," he meant plums.

Bolt said:

"Peace, greedygut!

"Plum-porridge is good, and bag-pudding is good, but put them together and they are filthy food."

Plum-pudding is oatmeal sweetened with plums.

"Bag-pudding" is a pudding boiled in an animal stomach or entrail. It is a kind of sausage.

In the slang of the time, a "plum" is a vulva, and a "bag" is a scrotum. And, yes, they can be brought together.

"Filthy food"? As food, yes. Figuratively, it can be quite good.

"Well, that's true," Sir Jeffrey Wiseacres said.

A wiseacre is someone who wants to be thought to be wise, but who is not wise.

"Right, sir," William Wallace said.

He set down the trunk he was carrying.

"What is this now?" Sir Jeffrey Wiseacres asked.

"Hunger is good, and two woodcocks are good, but the feathers of those two woodcocks must be plucked first," William Wallace said.

Woodcocks are proverbially foolish birds because they are easily caught. The two metaphorical "woodcocks" here are Sir Jeffrey Wiseacres and Bolt.

Fowl must be plunked — their feathers must be removed — before being cooked.

Fools are often plucked — that is, cheated.

Another meaning of the verb "pluck" is "humbled."

Yet another meaning is for a body part such as an arm to be taken hold of and pulled with a jerk.

William Wallace wanted to beat up and humiliate these two woodcocks.

"Stop, I order thee!" Sir Jeffrey Wiseacres said.

He was afraid of this man whom he did not know was William Wallace.

Using Scots dialect, William Wallace said, "Y'are a scurvy justice, yare man's an ass, and you another with a velvet footcloth on your back. I ken ye very well, and I'll knock ye very weel. If anything be worth victuals, it goes down here."

[You are a scurvy justice, your man's an ass, and you are another ass with a velvet footcloth on your back. I know what you are very well, and I'll knock you down very well. If anything is worth victuals, it goes down here.]

The horses of the upper class were caparisoned. On their backs were footcloths — long cloths hanging nearly to the ground. Here, Sir Jeffrey Wiseacres is an ass wearing the good clothing of a Justice of the Peace.

William Wallace was tired of being badly treated, and he wanted food — now. If anything — such as woodcocks — was edible, it was going to go down his throat — now.

Bolt said, "May the devil choke you, if you are a man of your word."

William Wallace said, "Wiseacres! If you would like to know who has gotten this trash — this bad treatment — from thee, it is I, Wallace the Scot."

Afraid, Sir Jeffrey Wiseacres and Bolt said, "Wallace!"

"Flee, Sir Jeffrey!" Bolt said. "He calls us woodcocks. Let's flee and raise the country!"

"Raise the country" meant to get the countrymen in the area to form a posse and hunt down and capture William Wallace.

William Wallace said:

"Do you grumble? Raise the devil and spare not!"

William Wallace was willing and ready to fight the devil.

Sir Jeffrey Wiseacres and Bolt ran away.

William Wallace said to the chest:

"Even if thou should turn out to be a chest full of gold, I'd give thee all away for victuals. Hunger, they say, will break stone walls. Your chops — your jaws — are not so hard; you shall burst, even if you were barred with iron ribs."

He opened the chest, looked inside, and said:

"Victuals; wine, too.

"Few justices feed the hungry like this.

"Of these justices who do not feed the poor, wiseacres are the most splendid fellows, especially English wiseacres."

Sir Jeffrey Wiseacres had unwittingly fed William Wallace. He had done that by running away, leaving the chest of food and wine behind.

A ragged man entered the scene. Recent years had not been kind to him, for he was miserably poor. He was also carrying a rope, a symbol of despair because people who had lost all hope sometimes hung themselves.

The ragged man said:

"I'll now be my own carver."

The three Fates commanded the pulse of life; they controlled human life. Clotho spun the thread of life. Lachesis measured the thread of life, determining how long a person lived. Atropos cut the thread of life; when the thread was cut, the person died.

The Fates gave each person a portion of life.

The ragged man was threatening to end his life, literally hanging himself and metaphorically carving — cutting — his thread of life.

In this society, "carving" meant cutting or slashing.

The ragged man continued:

"Misery and age, poverty and despair have brought me to death's door, and shall I not enter? Yes, I will. This key shall do it."

The key was the rope he was carrying. He could make a noose out of it and hang himself. This would open the door to the Land of the Dead.

The ragged man continued:

"Is Death so surly that a poor man may peak sooner with a king than speak with him when he has most need of him?

"Ugly, lean slave, as long as I may see him, there's no need for a grave."

Personified Death is commonly pictured as a skeleton: the leanest a body can be.

The ragged man did not care about a proper burial: He simply wanted to be dead.

"How are you now?" William Wallace asked. "What do thou look for?

"For that which a quarter of the world wants: a tree to be hanged upon," the ragged man said.

"Are thou weary of thy life?" William Wallace asked.

"Yes," the ragged man said. "All men are weary of their old wives. My life has gone up and down with me these threescore and odd years. It is time to be weary of it, I think, now."

All men are weary of their old wives? More likely, the men have grown old alongside their wives, and the men are impotent.

Possibly, the word "wives" is a typo for "lives."

"Up and down"? Bawdy, that, if "wives" is correct.

"And when thou have hanged thyself, whither do thou think thou will go then?" William Wallace asked.

"To the linen-draper," the ragged man said.

A linen-draper is a seller of linen.

"What linen-draper?" William Wallace asked.

The ragged man said:

"The richest in the world, my old grandmother, the earth. How many pairs of sheets has she had, do you think, since Adam and Eve lay together?"

This kind of sheet is literally a linen winding-sheet, used to wrap around a dead body to serve as a shroud.

Metaphorically, the ragged man's body would be wrapped in a covering — a shroud — of earth.

The ragged man continued:

"It's the best inn to lie at; a man shall be sure of good linen."

Earth is the best possible covering for a corpse.

"Who dwells hereabouts?" William Wallace asked.

"One upon whom all the poor in the country cry out," the ragged man said.

"Who's that?" William Wallace asked.

"Scarity, death, penury, famine, hunger," the ragged man answered. "I have not known that man lives by food these four days and therefore I'll descend to the antipodes because I'll kick at this world."

He had not eaten for four days.

The antipodes are on the opposite side of the world from the ragged man.

"Antipodes" etymologically means "having the feet opposite."

If someone from Great Britain and someone from Australia were to suddenly have the earth under their feet vanish, they would be standing sole to sole in the middle of the earth.

If the earth were to vanish from only the ragged man's feet, he would have to pass through the middle of the earth to get to the antipodes. According to Dante's *Inferno*, the center of the earth is the location of the ninth and last circle of the Land of the Dead.

Getting into the Land of the Dead is easy. Getting out? Not so much.

William Wallace said:

"Halt. Don't do it.

"Famine shall not kill thee; sit and eat thy belly full, drown thy cares in good wine.

"Because of my own fall, I pity others who are down."

The ragged man ate and drank.

William Wallace asked:

"Isn't it good cheer?"

"Cheer" is food and drink.

The ragged man said:

"It is splendid. I thank you for it.

"How many beggars does a rich man eat at his table at one meal, when those few crumbs are able to save a man's life?"

If a rich man's meal costs hundreds of dollars, and many, many people could be saved from a death by starvation if they each had a bowl of food that they can't get, how many poor people does the rich man eat at a single meal?

Donate to your local food pantry, y'all.

The ragged man continued:

"How did you come, sir, into this fearful nest of screech-owls and ravens?"

These are birds of ill omen.

"Cast up by the sea, I was shipwrecked and lost all my company of friends," William Wallace said.

The ragged man said:

"I wish that I had been one of them. I have lost more than you have done; I have lost all that I had except my sins and they bang so heavy on my eyelids I can scarcely look as high as the brims of my hat to heaven. I have such a mind downwards that I have almost forgotten who dwells over my head."

William Wallace said:

"Look up towards heaven. Don't be afraid, for no tyrant reigns there.

"I wish that thou had been with me at sea."

"So wish I," the ragged man said.

Wallace said in rhyming couplets:

"Had thou an atheist been and God not known,

"Thou would have found him in the deep; there he's best shown.

"He who at sea is shipwrecked and denies

"A deity (being there saved), damned lives and dies.

"Man, nowhere in the twinkling of an eye,

"Is thrown so near to hell or raised so high

"Towards heaven than when he's tossed upon the waves.

"It must be a hand omnipotent there that saves."

He then asked:

"But how did you come, sir, to be here?"

The ragged man answered, "I was banished from England (that does not grieve me), but I killed an old man; he was called Wallace."

He was referring to Old Wallace.

"Huh?" William Wallace said.

"Wallace," the ragged man said. "And I think he's still at my elbow."

William Wallace said:

"Elbow?"

He said to himself:

"This ragged man is Sir Thomas Selby, my father's murderer!"

William Wallace said out loud:

"Don't think upon it. Sit! Eat heartily!"

He said to himself:

"Thy last meal ..."

William Wallace said out loud:

"Sit down, I say!"

He said to himself:

"Never to rise again ..."

William Wallace said out loud:

"Drink wine!"

He said to himself:

"Drink deep, and let thy soul reel to hell."

Sir Thomas Selby said:

"I am almost dead with cold."

William Wallace said out loud:

"I'll fetch dry sticks and with two flints, kindle fire."

He said to himself:

"I'll beat out his brains.

"Oh, if medicine had the power to make thee young, I'd fetch thee drugs from the furthest points of the world and then I would arm thee or, into thy veins half of my own blood I'd pour, to lend thee strength so that I might kill thee nobly."

Sir Thomas Selby was now old and impoverished, and he had lost his vigor. If William Wallace and Sir Thomas Selby were to fight a duel now, it would be an unfair matchup. William Wallace would easily kill him.

"Be quiet," Sir Thomas Selby said. "I'll pay thee."

"What is this now?" William Wallace said.

Sir Thomas Selby's words did not seem to be addressed to him.

Sir Thomas Selby said:

"A slumber took me just now, and I thought that Old Wallace clapped me upon the shoulder with one hand and with the other he pointed to his wounds.

"At this I startled and spoke, but I don't know what.

"I'm cold at heart."

"I'll seek for fire," William Wallace said.

"I thank ye," Sir Thomas Selby said. "If what I utter, you tell to anyone, I am a dead man. You have me at your mercy and may betray me."

Sir Thomas Selby had confessed to murder.

William Wallace said:

"Not I. I won't tell anyone.

"Eat and get strength. I'll seek for fire."

He said to himself:

"Unless I am a devil (although I have cause to kill thee), yet my quick hand shall eschew it. Thy careless confidence does bind me to it.

"This mercy that I show now is for God's sake in partial payment of his mercy shown to me.

"If I should kill thee now, thou would owe me nothing. Live, and be still my debtor.

"I shall do thee more harm to give thee life than take it from thee.

"Heaven, in my father's blood who is chief share,

"Shall strike for me a revenge more just and fairer."

William Wallace exited.

Another ragged man entered the scene. He was Sir William Hazelrigg, and he was carrying apples.

Recognizing Sir Thomas Selby, Sir William Hazelrigg called:

"Selby! Selby!"

Seeing the chest of food, he said to himself:

"How like a churl thou eat alone, and thou are greedy to fatten misery."

"Here I am!" Sir Thomas Selby said.

"Look, I have found a jenneting tree," Sir William Hazelrigg said.

Jenneting trees produce a species of apples.

"Where does it stand?" Sir Thomas Selby asked.

"I'll not tell thee," Sir William Hazelrigg said. "Look, it's splendid food."

"Let me taste it," Sir Thomas Selby said.

"Not a paring," Sir William Hazelrigg said. "What do you have there?"

"The dole of plenty," Sir Thomas Selby said.

"Good old rogue, I thank thee," Sir Thomas Hazelrigg said. "I have a stomach like a lawyer. Let's eat fruit when we have filled our bellies."

"Not a bit," Sir Thomas Selby said.

"Huh," Sir William Hazelrigg said.

"Not a paring of cheese," Sir Thomas Selby said.

"I must eat," Sir William Hazelrigg said.

"Thou shall not," Sir Thomas Selby said. "I pay thee in thy own coin."

Hazelrigg had declined to let Selby eat apples, and now Selby was declining to let Hazelwood eat the food from the trunk.

"Thy doting age is almost at her journey's end," Sir William Hazelrigg said. "My youth, having far to go, needs more provision, and I'll have this —"

Sir William Hazelrigg was much younger than Sir Thomas Selby.

"Hands off!" Sir Thomas Selby said.

"You dog, you old devil!" Sir William Hazelrigg said.

He stabbed Sir Thomas Selby.

Sir Thomas Selby said:

"I thank thee. Thou have cut the thread in two of all my woes. May Heaven pardon us both.

"Adieu!"

He died.

Sir William Hazelrigg said:

"Selby, no water from the hallowed fount touched thee, thou are so fatal. Selby dead!"

According to Sir William Hazelrigg, Sir Thomas Selby was unlikely to go to Heaven.

Sir William Hazelrigg continued:

"God's building, which has stood this threescore years, this dagger has defaced; I wish that God's building — your body — were up again with ruin of my own."

He had killed the over-60-year-old Selby, but now he wished that Selby were alive and he was dead.

Sir William Hazelrigg continued:

"I never knew partners but one always the other overthrew.

"Thou and I did set up with one stock of care.

"I have undone and ruined thee, and now all's my share.

"It is not so sinful, nor so base a stroke,

"To spoil a willow as an old reverend oak.

"From me thou are gone, but I'll from hence never fly

"But sit by thee and sigh, and weep, and die."

Sir Jeffrey Wiseacres, Bolt, and some soldiers entered the scene.

Bolt ordered Sir William Hazelrigg, who had his back to him:

"Stand still!"

Bolt thought that Sir William Hazelrigg was William Wallace.

He then said to Jeffrey Wiseacres and the soldiers:

"That's he who turns his tail to us, which is as much as to say, 'A fart for your Worship.'"

"Down with him!" the soldiers said.

"Peace!" Jeffrey Wiseacres said. "Silence! It's a wild bull we came to set upon and therefore let those dogs that can, fasten bite soundly."

"My hearts, we don't come to bait — to torment — an ass in a bear's skin, but a lion in his own skin," Bolt said. "He's a traitor!"

"How do we know that?" Sir Jeffrey Wiseacres asked.

Bolt said:

"Because of this: He hides his face and we are not to back a traitor.

"Sir Jeffrey, will you get between me and the gallows if I strike him down?"

Bolt wanted Jeffrey Wiseacres to stop him from being hung if he (Bolt) killed William Wallace.

"I'll enter into a recognisance to hand, before thou shall hang," Sir Jeffrey Wiseacres said.

He would legally pledge to help Bolt and keep him from hanging.

"If you see my heart begin to faint, knock me down to put life into me," Bolt said.

"Fear nothing," Sir Jeffrey Wiseacres said.

Bolt gave Sir William Hazelrigg, whom he still thought was William Wallace, a mortal wound.

Sir William Hazelrigg said:

"Be damned! Both gods and men the act detest.

"Oh heaven, wipe this sin out for all the rest."

Both gods and men detest murder.

Sir William Hazelrigg's last words were a prayer that murder might vanish from the earth.

Or his words meant: Let this sin that is done to me wipe out all the sins that I have done.

He died.

"Your sins are wiped out, sir," Bolt said. "Your Scottish score is paid, sir."

Bolt and Sir Jeffrey Wiseacres still thought the dead man was William Wallace.

"Is he down?" Sir Jeffrey Wiseacres asked.

"He sprawls," Bolt said. "Wait! There's one asleep by him! Shall I kill the lice in his head, too?"

Killing the person would kill the lice because they would have no living blood to feed on.

Sir Jeffrey Wiseacres said:

"No! Don't wake a sleeping mastiff.

"The king's in the field; let's go posthaste to him.

"Bolt, thou shall be a knight as deep as myself for this manly deed. You shall be as much a knight as I am myself.

"As ye go through the country, cry aloud, 'The traitor's dead!'"

Bolt said, "Cry it out at the Cross and at the old Palace that Bolt was the man who brained and killed lusty — vigorous — Wallace."

Crosses were often placed at crossroads.

Everyone shouted, "The traitor's dead! The traitor's dead!"

They exited.

<h1 style="text-align:center">— 3.2. —</h1>

William Wallace returned, carrying dry sticks and straw, and two flints. He got ready to start a fire, and he beat the two flints together to create sparks to start the fire.

He said:

"Thou shall have fire soon, old man."

He noticed a corpse and said:

"Huh! Murdered?

"What should thou be? Who are you?"

He looked and then said:

"The face of Hazelrigg. It is he!"

He noticed the other corpse and then said:

"Just heavens! Ye have bestowed my duty upon someone else. Someone else killed him.

"I thank you because my blood does not stain my hand."

By "blood," he meant the violent shedding of blood.

He thanked Heaven because he did not have to murder Sir Thomas Selby and Sir William Hazelrigg to avenge the deaths of his father and his wife.

William Wallace continued:

"However both did die (whether in love and friendship or in hate), both shall together lie.

"The coffin you must sleep in is this cave,

"The whole heaven will be your winding sheet, all earth your grave.

"The early lark shall sadly ring your knell,

"Your dirge shall be sung by mournful Philomel."

Philomela was an Athenian princess who was raped by her sister's husband, Tereus, who cut out Philomela's tongue so that she could not tell anyone that he had raped her. Philomela, however, wove a tapestry. The tapestry contained pictures that told the story of the rape. When Procne, Philomela's sister, saw the tapestry and realized that her husband had raped her sister, she was so angry that she killed the son of her (Procne) and her husband, cooked him, and served him to her husband.

Procne and Philomela then fled from Tereus. To protect the two women from Tereus' anger, the gods turned Philomela into a nightingale and Procne into a swallow.

The song of the nightingale is sad.

William Wallace continued:

"Instead of flowers and strewing herbs, take these."

He scattered sticks over the two bodies.

William Wallace concluded:

"And, what my charity now fails to do,

"Poor robin-redbreast shall. My last adieu.

"I have other streams to swim. The rough or calm

"Venture, it is brave when danger's crowned with palm."

Robins were believed to scatter leaves and flowers over the bodies of dead men.

CHAPTER 4

— 4.1 —

The general of the Scottish forces met with Grimsby, Menteith, Comyn, and soldiers who were wearing blue caps. Drummers and flag-bearers were present. They were camping near Falkirk.

On 22 July 1298, the English and the Scots would fight the Battle of Falkirk.

"Upon this field-bed we will lodge this night," the Scottish general said. "The earth's a soldier's pillow. Here we pitch our tents."

"Up with our tents!" everyone said.

"Beat a drum to call people to council!" the Scottish general said.

A drummer played.

Grimsby advised the Scots to do something other than lodge there this night: fight the English army immediately.

He said:

"Beat the drum for action then, and not for words. Upon our spear points, our best counsel sits.

"Follow our best counsel, noble general; up with no tents if you dare regard me as worthy to advise, but with an easy, quiet march, move gently on."

"You speak against the scholarship and learning of war," the Scottish general said.

Grimsby replied:

"Now their beef-pots and their cans are tossed instead of pikes."

The English were tossing beef and liquor into their throats from beef-pots and drinking vessels.

Grimsby continued:

"Their arms are thrown about their wenches' middles — there's their close fight."

The English soldiers were "wrestling" wenches instead of fighting the Scots man-to-man.

Grimsby continued:

"Let us not lose the forelock in our hands."

Opportunity is personified as a woman with a forelock. Other than the forelock, she is bald. One must seize Opportunity by the forelock, for once she is past you, opportunity cannot be seized.

Grimsby continued:

"The English don't dream of us, yet we are as free-born as the English king himself; let's not be their slaves.

"Free Scotland or, in England, dig our graves!"

Shouts sounded: "À Wallace! À Wallace! À Wallace!"

This phrase meant, "Come to Wallace!"

Rugecrosse, a Scottish herald, entered the scene.

The Scottish general asked, "Rugecrosse, what cry is this?"

"It is the cry of the whole army, grown wild between joy and admiration — wonder — at the sight of Wallace."

"What!" all cried.

Rugecrosse said, "That dreadless, fearless soldier, for whom all Scotland shed a sea of tears as deep as that in which men thought him dead, sets, with his presence, all their hearts on fire who have just a sight of him."

Again, shouts were heard: "À Wallace! À Wallace!"

"Ask him to come here," Grimsby said.

Rugecrosse exited.

William Wallace entered the scene with drummers, colors (flags), and soldiers. Everyone embraced him.

"Do you hear the English march?" Comyn said. "They are at hand."

"Now Grimsby, they are using pikes as their tossing cans," the Scottish general said.

Cans are drinking vessels. The English, Grimsby had thought, were tossing liquor into their throats instead of being ready to throw spears or pikes at the enemy.

"I am glad our thunder wakes them," Grimsby said.

"Shall we go on?" Menteith asked.

The Scottish general asked, "Is it best to stop them in their march or to make a stand and confront them here?"

The choice was to go to the English army and fight or to wait here and fight the English army when it arrived.

"Make a stand!" all said.

The Scottish general then asked about a third option: "Or else retire back to the spacious plain for far more advantageous battle."

William Wallace said:

"And by so retiring be held to be runaways.

"Here stands my body, and before these English wolves stretch their jaws ever so wide, they from hence shall drive me."

In other words: The English soldiers shall have to drive me away before they open their jaws wide and devour Scotland.

William Wallace continued:

"I'll rather lie here fifty fathoms deep now, right this minute, than by retreating and giving back one foot of ground, prolong my life a thousand years."

"Then let us die or live here," the Scottish general said.

"Arm! Arm!" all said.

William Wallace said:

"Fall back? Not I! Death of myself is part.

"I myself will never flee, here's no false heart:

"Let's in our rising be or, in our falls,

"Like bells that ring alike at funerals

"As at coronations. Let each man meet his wound

"With the self-same joy as kings go to be crowned."

He then asked the Scottish general:

"Where will you be in charge?"

The Scottish general replied:

"I will be in charge of the battaile, the main body of troops.

"Valiant Grimsby is General of our Horse.

"Comyn commands the infantry.

"Menteith and you shall come up in the rear."

"The rear?" William Wallace asked.

"Yes!" the Scottish general said.

"No, sir! Let Menteith command the troops in the rear. Wallace shall not."

William Wallace did not want to command the rearguard. He wanted to lead the front troops: the vanguard.

"He may choose," the Scottish general said.

"He" was William Wallace. He could choose either to lead the rearguard with Menteith, or he could choose not to lead any troops.

The Scottish general had already assigned his officers their roles in the upcoming battle. This was no time to be making changes. To remove someone from a leadership position would be a grave insult.

William Wallace said:

"If I were to hunt within a wilderness a herd of tigers, I would scorn to cheat my glories from the sweat of others' brows by encountering the fierce beasts at secondhand when others' strength had tamed them. Let me meet the lion newly roused — flushed — from its lair, and when its eyes sparkle with flames of indignation.

"I have not, in the Academy of War, so often read chief lectures, now to come lag."

He meant that he had often been in the front lines, and he did not now want to be in the rear.

William Wallace continued:

"I'll have the leading of the vanguard, or none."

William Wallace wanted to lead the vanguard: the front troops. Or else he would lead no troops.

The Scottish general said, "Then none. You wrong us all. Men now are placed and must not be dishonored."

If one of the leaders were replaced now by William Wallace, that leader would be dishonored.

"So, dishonored," William Wallace said.

He felt that he was dishonored.

"Charge in the rear, for God's sake!" the Scottish general said. "To stand now on terms of worth hazards the fate of all."

The Scottish general was right. Personal feelings of honor needed to be set aside for the good of Scotland.

William Wallace said:

"Well, so be it then, the rear. Do you see yonder hill?

"Yonder I'll stand, and although I should see butchers cut all your throats like sheep, I will not stir until I see the proper time myself."

The proper time to stir and fight would be *before* his fellow soldiers in the vanguard had their throats cut like sheep.

The Scottish general said:
"Your pleasure.
"Onward! Each leader employ his best direction."

King Edward I, Percy, Robert Bruce, Hertford, Sir Jeffrey Wiseacres, and Bolt met together. Drummers and flag-bearers were present.

The time was just before the Battle of Falkirk. News had been brought to King Edward I that William Wallace was dead.

"Which is the fellow who killed him?" King Edward I asked.

"I am the party, sir," Bolt said.

"Stand forth before the king," Percy said.

Sir Jeffrey Wiseacres said to Bolt about the king, "He's no sheep-biter."

Sheep-biters are dogs that bite sheep instead of protecting them.

Bolt moved closer to the king.

"Did thou kill Wallace?" King Edward I asked Bolt.

"Yes, by the Virgin Mary, I did, sir," Bolt said. "Even if I should be hanged here before you, I would not deny it."

"How did thou kill him?" King Edward I asked. "Hand to hand?"

"Hand to hand, as dog-killers kill dogs," Bolt said. "So I beat out his brains, I'm sure."

In this society, stray dogs were sometimes clubbed to death.

"I think that thou would not look him in the face," King Edward I said.

He thought that Bolt would be afraid to face William Wallace.

"No more I did," Bolt said. "I came behind his back and felled him."

"Are thou a gentleman?" King Edward I asked.

"I am no gentleman born," Bolt said. "My father was a poor fletcher in Grubstreet, but I am a gentleman by my position."

A fletcher is a dealer in arrows. He may make bows and arrows.

"What position is that?" King Edward I asked.

"I am the clerk of a Justice of the Peace: Sir Jeffrey Wiseacres," Bolt answered.

"My serving-man, this clerk, if it please your Majesty, is an honest and true knave," Sir Jeffrey Wiseacres said.

"Give to Sir Wiseacres' clerk a hundred pounds!" King Edward I ordered.

"I thank your grace," Sir Jeffrey Wiseacres said.

"May God confound all your foes at the same rate!" Bolt said.

In other words: May other people who kill your foes also receive a hundred pounds.

"But if this Wallace, sirrah, is found to be alive now, you and your hundred pounds shall both be hanged," King Edward I said to Bolt.

Bolt may have been a small man who weighed a hundred pounds.

Bolt agreed:

"I will be hanged before I part from my money."

He then asked:

"Who pays me? Who pays me?"

Clifford entered the scene and said, "Charge! Charge!"

"What is the news, brave Clifford?" King Edward I asked.

"The daring Scots, fuller of insolence than strength, stand forth to bid us to battle," Clifford replied.

Clifford was an experienced and competent military man. If he said that the Scots were "fuller of insolence than strength," he ought to be believed.

King Edward I said:

"Throw defiance back down their throats, and of our heralds, Northumberland, the honor shall be thine."

Percy was the Earl of Northumberland.

King Edward I continued:

"Tell them we come to scourge their pride with whips of steel. Their city has from justice snatched her sword to strike their sovereign, who has turned the point upon their own breasts."

The *country* of Scotland had rebelled against the king. King Edward I may be using the word "city" to minimize the extent of the rebellion.

King Edward I concluded:

"Tell them this."

"I shall," Percy said.

He exited.

"Where's noble Bruce?" Clifford asked.

"Here!" Robert Bruce said.

Clifford said:

"I have a message, but it is more honorable, sent to you, too: The herald says that Wallace dares you. His spite is all at you, and if your spirit and mettle are as great as his, you will find him in the rear."

William Wallace was daring Robert Bruce to come to him.

Part of the content of his message was this: William Wallace was still alive, despite what Bolt had said.

"Hang up that Wiseacres, and the fool his man!" King Edward I said.

In this society, "the fool his man" can mean "the fool's man." In this case, since Bolt was a fool, that could mean "the man the fool serves," and so the king was saying twice, "Hang up that Wiseacres."

Or, since Wiseacres was also a fool, "the fool's man" could mean "the fool's serving-man," aka Bolt.

"My master, not me, Sir!" Bolt said. "I have a legal recognisance from him to stand between me and the gallows."

"A king's word must be kept," King Edward I said. "Hang them both!"

"One word more, good sir, before I go to this business," Bolt said. "If a king's word must be kept, why was it not kept when he gave me the hundred pounds? Wipe out one, I'll wipe out the other."

In other words: You keep the one hundred pounds, and my master and I will keep our lives.

"That jest has saved your lives," King Edward I said. "Let me see you fight today."

It wasn't much of a jest, but King Edward I had more important matters at hand. He had a war to fight, and a couple of extra soldiers would be welcome if they fought well — and if these particular soldiers did not fight well, they might die in battle.

"We will fight bravely, like cocks," Sir Jeffrey Wiseacres said.

One meaning of "cock" is "rooster."

According to the *Oxford English Dictionary*, another meaning of "cock" is "A conical heap of hay, grass, etc."

"Now, Wallace, look after your coxcomb," Bolt said.

Roosters had coxcombs. So did Fools. And some plants had flowers that resembled the coxcomb of a cock.

"Move on!" all said.

Some Scottish soldiers entered the scene, but they were fought off.

"We have fleshed them soundly!" King Edward I said.

One meaning of "to flesh" is "to gratify destructive rage."

Another meaning is to feed a dog or a hawk flesh to make it more eager to hunt.

The Scottish soldiers had wanted a fight, and they had gotten one.

"I would not wish to meet with braver spirits," Clifford said.

"Wait, Bruce!" King Edward I said. "What's yonder on the hill?"

"They are colors: Scottish flags," Bruce replied.

"Why do they mangle thus their army's limbs?" King Edward I said. "What's that doing so far off?"

The Scottish soldiers on the hill were doing nothing while the vanguard was fighting and dying. The limbs of the Scottish army were mangled because an important part of their army was not fighting.

"Surely, it is the rearguard," Robert Bruce said, "where burns the black brand that kindles all this fire: I mean the traitor Wallace."

King Edward I said:

"What! Has he turned coward? A dog of so good mouth and stand at bay?"

Some dogs barked loudly but were afraid to fight the prey.

King Edward I continued:

"If in this heat of fight we break their ranks, then press through and charge that devil, Bruce thyself!"

"To hell if I can chase him," Robert Bruce said.

King Edward I said:

"Charge up strong! Listen, brave and defy and fight the Scots. Let now our hands be warriors, not our tongues!"

The Scottish general, Grimsby, Comyn, and Menteith talked together in the presence of the Scottish army.

A cry sounded: "They flee! They flee!"

"The English shrink," the Scottish general said. "Let's knit all our nerves, strengthen our resolution, and fasten fortune's offer.

"Keep steady footing," Grimsby said. "The day is lost if you stir. Don't stir, but do withstand the tempest of battle."

In other words: Hold your ground, and don't advance.

"I cry we go on!" Comyn said.

"And I!" the Scottish general said.

They wanted to advance.

"So I do not!" Grimsby said. "This starting back — this retreat — is only an English earthquake, which to dust shakes rotten towers but builds the sound towers stronger."

"Let's continue onward, and dare death in the thickest throng," the Scottish general said.

They advanced, and English soldiers appeared and surrounded the Scots.

"Didn't I give you warning of this whirlpool for going too far?" Grimsby asked.

Odysseus sailed between Scylla and Charybdis in Homer's *Odyssey*. Scylla was a monster with six heads, each of which could grab one of his men, and Charybdis was a whirlpool that could swallow his ship, him, and the men who served him.

"We are all dead men," Menteith said. "Yet fight as long as legs and arms last."

Arms are 1) body appendages, and 2) weapons.

King Edward I said:

"In how quick time have we built a wall of brass around you!

"How is it that he, whom here you call your general, has been a soldier considered remarkable and of great education, and yet now he is caught with a simple trick like a bird caught with lime twigs?"

Lime twigs are a trap: Branches were covered with sticky birdlime to trap birds.

"Keep our ground!" the Scottish general said.

"If we must fall, fall bravely," Grimsby said.

"Wound for wound," Menteith said.

War trumpets sounded.

King Edward I and Robert Bruce exited, pursuing some of the Scots.

Clifford and Percy stayed behind, confronting Grimsby and the Scottish general.

Clifford said:

"Take breath! I don't want to have the world robbed of two such spirits."

"Spirits" are 1) spirited, brave men, and 2) souls.

The spirits were Grimsby and the Scottish general.

Clifford then said to a messenger:

"Hasten to the king and tell him that the noblest hearts of the whole herd are hunted to the toil: the snare. Ask whether they shall fall or shall live for gain."

If they lived, they could be ransomed for money.

"I shall," the messenger said.

He exited.

Someone cried, "Charge!"

Menteith appeared and shouted to William Wallace, "For honor's sake, come down from the hill and save thy country!"

"Whose is the day?" William Wallace asked.

He was asking who had won.

"The day is Edward's!" Menteith said, "Come rescue our general and the noble Grimsby."

"Who?" William Wallace asked.

"Our general and stout Grimsby are surrounded with quick-sets made of steel," Menteith said. "Come fetch them off or all is lost."

Quick-sets are living bushes — especially bushes with thorns — that form hedges.

The Scottish general and Grimsby were surrounded by hedges made of English soldiers wielding steel weapons.

"Is the day lost?" William Wallace asked.

"Lost, lost," Menteith said.

"Unless the day is quite lost, I will not stir," William Wallace said.

"It is quite lost," Menteith said.

"Why then descend amain?" William Wallace said. "Are thou sure the day — the battle — is lost?"

"Amain" means 1) with all our might, and 2) as fast as possible.

"Yes," Menteith said.

"Then we'll win it again!" William Wallace said.

Wallace's plan was much the same as Achilles' plan in Book 9 of Homer's *Iliad*. Achilles was dishonored by Agamemnon, leader of the Greek forces, and so he withdrew from fighting. Instead of fighting alongside the soldiers whom he had brought to Troy, he and his soldiers would keep out of the battle and let the Trojans win. Only when the Trojans set fire to the Greek camp and the fires reached his own tent and the tents of his soldiers would he and his soldiers fight the Trojans and drive them back to Troy. That way, Agamemnon would be humiliated, and Achilles would be a victor. That was the plan.

Achilles' plan worked out badly, and his best friend, Patroclus, died.

A messenger entered the scene and went to Clifford.

"What is the news now?" Clifford asked.

"The king proclaims that man a traitor who saves, when he may kill," the messenger said.

In other words: Kill all the Scots! Take no prisoners!

Clifford said:

"Charge them! Black day!

"The lion hunts a lion for his prey."

A fight ensued. More English soldiers and more Scottish soldiers, including Sir John Graham, appeared and fought.

William Wallace and his soldiers appeared and fought off the English soldiers. They found Sir John Graham dead and the Scottish general wounded.

Alone, Robert Bruce entered the scene.

The Scottish general said, "Too late!"

He died.

William Wallace said:

"Why then, farewell! I'll make what haste I can to follow thee.

"Bruce! Bruce! I am here: It is Wallace who calls thee, dares thee!"

This sounded like a challenge to fight man-to-man, but William Wallace's sword was not raised in anger; instead, it drooped.

Robert Bruce said:

"Although I never stooped to a traitor's lure, I scorn thine."

Falconers used a feathered decoy — a lure — to recall falcons. When a falcon stoops, aka swoops, it descends swiftly. It can descend swiftly on either its prey or its lure.

If Robert Bruce were to stoop to a lure, he would know what that lure was.

Robert Bruce scorned William Wallace's lure without even knowing what it was.

Robert Bruce continued:

"Why do thou single out me yet turn thy weapon downward to the earth?"

When one soldier singles out another soldier, it is usually to fight them one-on-one.

A dare is a challenge, but William Wallace was not challenging Robert Bruce to single combat; instead, he would challenge Robert Bruce to rise to the occasion and become King of the Scots.

"Let's catch our breath, rest, and talk," William Wallace said.

"I'll parley with no traitor except with blows," Robert Bruce said.

A parley is a conversation between enemies.

"You shall have blows, your guts full," William Wallace said. "I'm no traitor."

"Why against thy sovereign do thou lift then thy sword?" Robert Bruce asked.

"You see I am not lifting it," William Wallace said.

"Tell Edward, thy king, that," Robert Bruce said.

William Wallace said:

"Edward Longshanks was never sovereign of mine, nor shall he be while Bruce lives."

King Edward I was called "Longshanks" because he was tall.

William Wallace was saying that Robert Bruce, not Edward Longshanks, was his sovereign.

William Wallace continued:

"Thou are but bastard English, for thou are Scotch true born. Thou are made a mastiff among a herd of wolves to weary those whom thou should be the shepherd of."

Metaphorically, Robert Bruce was a sheepdog that attacked instead of guarding the sheep. Literally, he was a Scot who ought to be the King of Scots but instead attacked other Scots.

William Wallace continued:

"The fury of the battle now declines; take my counsel, although I seem to be thy foe.

"Wash both thy hands in blood and when soon the English in their tents boast about their deeds, lift thy bloody hands up, and boast about your deeds, and with a sharp eye note with what scorn the English repay thy merit."

"This I'll try," Robert Bruce said.

"Do thou dare to meet me alone in Glasgow Moor?" William Wallace said. "There I'll tell thee more."

"Thou will have no treason towards me?" Robert Bruce asked.

He was asking if this was a trap.

"Here's my hand," William Wallace said. "I am as clear as innocence. Had I meant treason, here I could work it on thee. I have none."

They shook hands.

"In Glasgow Moor I'll meet thee," Robert Bruce said. "Fare thee well."

"The time?" William Wallace asked.

"Some two hours hence," Robert Bruce said.

"There I will untie a knot, at which hangs death or sovereignty," William Wallace said.

He was saying that he would explain a situation that could lead to Robert Bruce either dying (perhaps involving hanging) or to his becoming King of Scots.

They exited.

— 4.4. —

Several people talked together in the English camp at Falkirk.

"We have sweat hard today," King Edward I said.

"It was a brave — a splendid — hunting," Clifford said.

Bolt placed his coat before the king so the king could stand on it, but the king did not stand on it.

King Edward I said:

"Sit! Some wine! Away in the battlefield, all are fellows."

The English soldiers had fought well, and all were comrades-at-arms. They were a band of brothers.

King Edward I then asked:

"Whose coat is this?"

"It was my coat at arms, but now it is yours at legs," Bolt answered.

"Take it away! Why do thou give me a cushion?" King Edward I said.

"Because of the two of us, I take you to be the better man," Bolt said.

King Edward I said:

"A soldier's coat shall never be so base as to lie beneath my heel. Thou are in this place my fellow and companion.

"A health to all in England!"

"Let it come!" all said.

In other words: Let the toast of health and happiness become reality to all in England.

"Isn't this he who killed Wallace?" Clifford asked.

"No, sir, I am only he who said so," Bolt said. "As you sit, so did I lie."

Attention: Pun alert.

"Sirrah, where's your master?" King Edward I asked.

"My master is shot," Bolt said.

"What! Shot? Where?" King Edward I asked.

"In the back," Bolt said.

"Oh, he ran away," Clifford said.

"No, my Lord, but his harness cap was blown off and he, running after it to catch it, was shot between the neck and shoulders and, when he stood upright, he had two heads," Bolt said.

A harness cap is a helmet or an armored cap. Since they are heavy, they are unlikely to blow off.

"Two heads?" King Edward I asked. "How?"

Bolt said:

"Yes, truly. His own head and the arrowhead."

He added:

"It was twenty to one that I had not been shot before him."

A twenty to one is a long shot: an unlikely outcome. Bolt was saying that it was unlikely that he had not been shot before Wiseacres was shot. In other words, the expected outcome of the battle was that he would have been shot before Wiseacres was shot.

"Why, I ask?" King Edward I said.

Bolt answered:

"Because my knight's name is Wiseacres and my name is Bolt, and you know a fool's bolt is soon shot."

A "wiseacre" is a fool, and Bolt served Sir Jeffrey Wiseacres, and therefore Bolt was a fool's bolt.

A bolt is an arrow. Fools shoot their arrows at the enemy before the enemy comes close enough to be shot.

"He has pinned the title of 'fool' upon his master's shoulder very handsomely," Clifford said.

"Sirrah, go seek your master and bid him take measures for the burying of the dead," King Edward I ordered Bolt.

"I shall, sir," Bolt said, "and while he takes orders for the burials of the dead, I'll take measures for the stomachs of the living."

He would find something to eat.

"How did our English fight today?" King Edward I asked.

"Bravely," Percy said.

"How did the Scots fight?" King Edward I asked.

Clifford said:

"The pangs of war are similar to child-bed throes — labor pains — bitter in suffering, but the storm being past, the talk, like talk about an escape from shipwreck, tastes sweet.

"The death of the Scotch general went to my heart. He had in him of manhood as much as any man and for all I think, his blood was poorly sold by his own countrymen, rather than bought by us. "

In other words: He died because his soldiers fought so poorly, rather than because we fought so well.

Clifford continued:

"If the rearguard, where Wallace did command, had not stood and given aim, it would have been a day bloody and dismal, and whose day it would have been is hard to say."

"To stand and give aim" means "to stand near the target and tell the shooter where he had gone wrong." E.g.: shoot short of the target, overshoot the target, shoot to the right or the left of the target. To give aim is a form of criticism.

If William Wallace and his soldiers had not stood and given aim (criticized the Scottish general and his soldiers) but had instead charged and fought in support of the Scottish general and his soldiers, then perhaps the Scottish army might have won the battle.

"Giving aim" is also a form of helping.

By not fighting until it was too late for the Scots to win the battle, William Wallace had helped the English soldiers win the battle.

Clifford continued:

"Sir, you shall give me leave to drink a health to all the valiant Scots."

He wanted to drink a toast to the brave Scots who had fought well in the battle but had lost.

"Clifford, I'll pledge thee," King Edward I said. "Give me my bowl of wine."

He drank.

"Sir, I remembered Wallace in my draught," Clifford said.

"I did not," King Edward I said. "If this cup were Wallace's skull, I'd drink it full with blood, for it would save the lives of thousands."

If the English could kill William Wallace, an important leader of the Scots, many lives would be saved.

"I, for all your kingdoms, would not pledge it so," Clifford said.

"I would, no matter how a traitor falls," Percy said.

"Percy, ten thousand crowns would buy that traitor's head, if I could have it for money," King Edward I said.

Crowns are coins.

Clifford said:

"I would give twice twenty thousand crowns to have his head on my sword's point, cut from him with this arm.

"But how? On the battlefield, nobly, hand to hand.

"I would not give this straw to a hangman who would bring it to me."

King Edward I said:

"Let that pass. Let's talk about something else.

"Where's Robert Bruce, our noble Earl of Carrick?"

"I haven't seen him today," Percy said.

Clifford said:

"I did, and I saw his sword, as if it were a reaper's scythe, mow down the Scots."

Robert Bruce entered the scene.

Clifford said:

"Here he comes!"

King Edward I said:

"You have splendid armor: a rampant lion within a field all gules."

"Gules" is the heraldic term for red. The Scottish royal coat of arms depicts a red lion rampant — a red lion standing on its hind legs. The field — background color — of the Scottish royal coat of arms is gold.

King Edward I then asked:

"Where have you been, Bruce?"

"Following the execution that we held, three English miles in length," Robert Bruce said.

He and others had chased after the retreating Scots for three miles.

An English mile is 1.6 km; an old Scottish mile was 1.8 km.

King Edward I said:

"Give him some wine!

"Aren't you thirsty?"

Robert Bruce replied:

"Yes, I am thirsty for Scottish blood. I never shall have enough of it.

"I drink to the king's health!"

"Let come!" all said, and they drank.

In other words: May the toast bring health to the king.

"How greedily yonder Scot drinks his own blood!" Percy said.

Some Englishmen laughed.

"If he should taste your bitterness, it would not be well," King Edward I said to Percy.

Such a bitter joke could lead to a fight.

"What's that you all laughed at?" Robert Bruce asked.

"Nothing but a jest," Clifford said, wanting to keep the peace.

"Nay, good sir, tell me," Robert Bruce asked.

Wanting to keep the peace, King Edward I said:

"It was an idle jest.

"More wine for Bruce!"

"No more, I have drunk too much," Robert Bruce said, adding, "Wallace and I did parley."

The two had talked together.

"How, in words?" Percy asked.

Robert Bruce lied:

"No, Percy. I'm no prattler — no chatterer. It was with swords."

He then asked:

"Your laughing jest was not at me?"

"No, sir!" all lied.

"Bruce would fain — would eagerly — quarrel," King Edward I said.

"I have done, sir," Robert Bruce said. "I have finished."

A trumpet sounded.

"Peace!" King Edward I said. "What trumpet is that?"

"It's from the enemy, surely," Clifford said.

"Go and find out!" King Edward I ordered.

Before Clifford could leave, Rugecrosse, a Scottish herald, entered the scene.

"I come from William Wallace," Rugecrosse said.

"So, sir, what about him?" King Edward I asked.

Rugecrosse answered:

"Thus he speaks:

"He bids me dare you to a fresh battle by tomorrow's sun, army to army, troop to troop, he challenges; or, to save blood, a battle of fifty English soldiers against fifty Scottish soldiers shall decide the strife, or a single combat of one against one."

King Edward I said:

"A herald to the traitor!

"Go and thus speak:

"We bring whips of steel to scourge rebellion, not to stand the braves — endure the boasts — of a base daring vassal.

"Tell him that before that sun which he calls for has risen, pay it and save his country and himself from ruin."

In other words: Before the sunrise that William Wallace has called for, he needs to pay the Sun — King Edward I — what he owed.

According to King Edward I, William Wallace owed him his loyalty.

King Edward I continued:

"Charge him on his head to make his quick submission."

In other words: Tell him that he must either submit to the king or lose his head.

King Edward I continued:

"If he slows the minutes and delays his submission to me, we'll proclaim in thunder his and his country's ruin.

"Go, be gone!"

He then told his soldiers:

"Arm!"

"Arm! Arm!" all his soldiers said.

King Edward I said:

"A land that's sick at heart must take sharp pills,

"For dangerous physic — dangerous medicine — best cures dangerous ills."

Everyone exited.

CHAPTER 5

— 5.1 —

Robert Bruce and Clifford talked together in the English camp.

"As you are a soldier, as you are noble," Robert Bruce said, "I charge you and conjure you — and entreat you — to unclasp a book in which I am graveled."

"Graveled" meant "perplexed."

Robert Bruce was wondering what he should do.

"Perhaps I cannot," Clifford said.

"Yes, you can," Robert Bruce said. "If you dare, you can."

"Dare?" Clifford said. "Clifford dares do anything except wrong and what's not just."

"Then tell me, sir, what was that bitter scorn which I, like poison, tasted in my wine?" Robert Bruce asked.

Clifford answered, "I don't care if I tell you because I love virtue, even in my enemy. Seeing the bowl of wine kissing your lip, someone said, 'How eagerly yonder Scot drinks his own blood.'"

"Yonder Scot drinks his own blood?" Robert Bruce asked. "Which Scot?"

"You had best awaken some oracle," Clifford said.

An oracle is a wise person who can answer questions. Some oracles are priests or priestesses who channel the answers of a god.

"Who broke the jest upon me?" Robert Bruce asked, realizing that he was the Scot. "Who ridiculed me with a joke?"

"Please pardon me," Clifford said, unwilling to answer, lest Percy and Robert Bruce fight a duel.

Clifford exited.

Alone, Robert Bruce said to himself:

"The oracle I'll awaken is here."

He would be his own oracle and find his own answers.

He continued:

"Oh, Wallace, I never had eyes until now. Before, they were closed by braving, boasting, threatening English witchcraft.

"'Drinks his own blood.'

"England, my stepdame, take my bitter curse: May thy own fingernails tear thy own bowels."

In fairy tales, stepmothers have a reputation for being cruel.

Robert Bruce continued:

"Oh, my parent, dear Scotland, I no more will be a goad pricking thy sides, but if I ever draw a sword, it shall be double-edged with blood and fire to burn and drown this kingdom and this king."

A gentleman entered the scene and said, "My general ordered me to give you these in privacy."

Realizing from whom the articles had come, Robert Bruce said:

"Thanks, noble Clifford."

He then asked:

"What did he tell thee to say?"

"To say nothing, but just to do this," the gentleman said.

The gentleman exited.

Clifford had sent Robert Bruce an oracle. The message lay in the articles he had sent to Robert Bruce.

Looking at the items, Robert Bruce said to himself:

"A pair of spurs? Bruce never was a runaway.

"Twelve silver pence. Oh, bitter scorn, with Judas I have betrayed my master, my dear country; and here's the emblem of my treachery, to hasten to some tree and, desperate, die."

Matthew 26:14-15 (King James Version) states:

14 Then one of the twelve, called Judas Iscariot, went unto the chief priests,

15 And said unto them, What will ye give me, and I will deliver him unto you? And they covenanted with him for thirty pieces of silver.

16 And from that time he sought opportunity to betray him.

Matthew 27:3-5 (King James Version) states:

3 Then Judas, which had betrayed him, when he saw that he was condemned, repented himself, and brought again the thirty pieces of silver to the chief priests and elders,

4 Saying, I have sinned in that I have betrayed the innocent blood. And they said, What is that to us? see thou to that.

5 And he cast down the pieces of silver in the temple, and departed, and went and hanged himself.

Robert Bruce's first thought was that the message of the gift was ignoble. Spurs indicated that he ran away. Pieces of silver indicated that he had sold out his country. Therefore, the message was that he had run away from his people and had sold them out.

Robert Bruce continued with a different interpretation of the oracle:

"Twelve sterling silver pence. Sterling, ha! Stirling — it is a limb of Scotland. Spurs for flight."

His second thought was that the gift was advice. The spurs indicated that he should go somewhere. The silver was sterling (92 and one-half percent pure) silver, and Stirling is a county in central Scotland. Also, the Scots had won a significant victory in the Battle of Stirling Bridge. Therefore, the message was that he should go to the Scottish army and help his people.

Robert Bruce concluded:

"Clifford, I'll go hither, whether my commentary — my interpretation — is wrong or right."

An oracle can be an answer to some pressing question by some priest or priestess channelling a god. Oracles can be ambiguous.

Apollo shot arrows and killed the Python, a serpent, at Delphi, which is located on a spur of Mount Parnassus, and he then made Delphi the site of his own oracle. When Croesus, the King of Lydia, was thinking about attacking Persia, he asked the Delphic Oracle what he should do. The Oracle said, "If you attack Persia, a mighty kingdom will fall." Croesus attacked Persia, and a mighty kingdom did fall: the kingdom of Lydia.

The Delphic oracle was right whether Lydia won the war or Persia won the war.

Robert Bruce would accept the Clifford Oracle's advice whether he stayed and helped the English or he went to the Scottish army and helped the Scots.

Grimsby, Menteith, Comyn, an English herald, and Rugecrosse talked together in the English camp near Glasgow Moor.

"Wait, noble Grimsby. Before the English herald further passes, one of us ought to certify — notify — our general," Menteith said. "Perhaps he won't admit him into his presence."

William Wallace was the Scottish general.

"That is likely," Grimsby said. "Let's delay the English herald here. I will take the responsibility for it."

"Let Rugecrosse bring his pleasure," Comyn said.

In other words: Let Rugecrosse, the Scottish herald, go to the Scottish general and bring back the information about what the general wants.

"Come, agreed," Grimsby said.

Grimsby and Rugecrosse exited.

"You bring from Longshanks some strange message now?" Menteith asked the English herald.

"At least he sends his gauntlet," Comyn said.

Throwing down a gauntlet was a challenge to a duel.

A gauntlet is a glove that protects the hand and wrist in battle. It is made of metal plates or hardened leather.

Menteith said:

"Gauntlet? No!

"The English don't fight two days together, but like swaggerers, a fray being settled with a wound or so, the man whose throat should have been cut earlier is now a sworn brother."

He said to the English herald:

"Now that we have mauled your nation, they'll fawn on us like spaniels, won't they?"

Some years had passed since the English had decisively won the Battle of Falkirk.

"And that's thy errand, isn't it?" Comyn asked the English herald.

Menteith said to the English herald:

"Commonly, when the English see that they are too weak at fighting, they resort to fishing and then bait the hook with mercy and the king's pardon, and whoever bites at that has his swallowing spoiled for ever.

"There's no Scot but scorns to hand his hope on your king's promises, no matter how those promises smoothly gild his hope."

"He gilds none, sir," the English herald said.

"I warrant — I guarantee — he would pawn half his dominions to shake hands with Wallace and be friends," Menteith said.

"If King Edward I just had William Wallace in his court, he would outshine his capering — dancing — gallants. He would dote on him, as Jupiter did on Ganymede, and he would make him his chief minion — his chief favorite," Comyn said.

Jupiter, the king of the gods, fell in love with a beautiful boy named Ganymede, so he kidnapped him and made him his cupbearer and let him pour his wine.

"He already does so," the English herald said. "He really does 'dote' upon him. It is not yet the age of one hour since my master swore to give ten thousand crowns to any Scot or Englishman who would be so bold as to bring him Wallace's head."

Rudecrosse returned and said, "The English herald."

Rudecrosse and the English herald exited so the herald could deliver his message to William Wallace.

"Ten thousand crowns?" Sir John Menteith said.

"They would make a fair show in our purse, Jack," Comyn said.

"I could pick out five thousand heads who would boldly dare to sell William Wallace at that rate," Menteith said.

He would get five thousand coins, each of which would have a portrait of a notable's head on it.

Together, they would get ten thousand crowns for handing Wallace over to the English. Of course, King Edward I wanted to execute William Wallace.

"Ten thousand crowns?" Comyn said.

Menteith said:

"Aye, and court windfalls, too. Some English earldom or such.

"Here is none but friends; should you betray this conversation, I don't care. I would deny it, and I would oversway your evidence against me no matter how massive."

He was broaching the subject of turning over William Wallace to the English so that they could get money and titles.

"It shall not be necessary to worry about me reporting this conversation," Comyn said. "Believe me, worthy Menteith, what you lock here in my heart is safe."

"Shall we earn this English gold, this ten thousand crowns?" Menteith asked.

"Here is my hand," Comyn said.

They shook hands.

"The ten thousand crowns are ours," Menteith said. "He's dead."

"Say no more!" Comyn said. "He comes!"

William Wallace, Grimsby, and the English herald entered the scene.

William Wallace said to the English herald:

"I am to him no vassal; he's a tyrant.

"So tell him: Before his frown shall cause me to bend my knee, this body of mine shall be hanged upon the gallows 'tree.'

"As for my appearance, tell him this; I'll dine on Christmas Day next in his English court and in his great hall at Westminster, at his own table. We'll drink Scotch healths in his standing cups of gold. His black jacks, hand in hand, about his court, shall march with our blue bonnets."

Standing cups have a base on which they stand.

Blackjacks are leather mugs coated in tar, and blue bonnets are blue caps worn by the Scots.

William Wallace continued:

"We'll eat nothing but what our swords shall carve, so tell his soldiers we'll sit like lords there while they rail and disapprove like slaves.

"Go with Scotch threats to pay back your English braves!"

English "braves" are English boasts.

The English herald exited.

"You'll make the English mad," Grimsby said.

"A brave defiance," Menteith said.

William Wallace said:

"Defiance? Let's madden them more; they shall not sleep tonight.

"Good Grimsby, beat a drum! Let bonfires shine through all our army as if our tents were burnt and we were dislodged; but re-collect our troops into an ordered body.

"Some thing we'll do to make our chronicles — our histories — swell with English rue."

The "thing" they would do was not specified, but William Wallace was definitely making a threat.

"A drum!" Grimsby said. "Call a drum!"

Grimsby exited.

William Wallace said, "Oh, Sir John Menteith, I have cracked the ice to — I have began — a design, aka plan, which, if it will succeed, England no more shall strike, and Scotland no more shall bleed."

"Let's be partakers, dear sir," Menteith and Comyn said.

"What will you say if I win Robert Bruce from the English side and persuade him to join our side?" William Wallace asked.

"That would be the happiest day that ever shone on Scotland," Menteith said.

"And crown Robert Bruce King of the Scots?" Comyn asked.

William Wallace said:

"That's the upshot that must crown all."

Literally, an upshot is the final shot in an archery contest. Figuratively, an upshot is a conclusion or final result.

He continued:

"I'm to meet him in Glasgow Moor before one hour grows old."

"How will you meet him?" Menteith asked.

"As I am," William Wallace said. "Both of us will come alone. Say no words to anyone about this."

"Our lips are sealed," Menteith said.

"Will you ride or go on foot?" Comyn asked.

"I'll go no more on foot," William Wallace said. "I'll ride."

Sir John Menteith said to himself, "We'll pass the wood on foot."

"Jack Menteith, I laugh to think what face Longshanks will make, when he shall hear what guests will dine with him in his court on Christmas Day," William Wallace said.

"What face?" Menteith said. "He'll kill the herald, for sure."

"Oh!" William Wallace said. "I need some charm for me to be invisible there and see him."

Menteith whispered to Comyn, "For my part of ten thousand crowns, by this hand I wish William Wallace to be there in the court."

"And for as many of mine, I swear," Comyn whispered to Menteith.

Menteith whispered to Comyn:

"The time may come.

"In his exchequer — his treasury — we may share twice that sum."

Whose treasury? Were they expecting to get more money from the Scottish treasury if Scotland were to fall to England?

"Go hence!" William Wallace said. "Hurry and go before me. Keep close — hidden and quiet — in the wood. Break forth in shouts if you spy treason. If you don't spy treason, don't shout."

"Good," Menteith and Comyn said.

Menteith and Comyn exited.

Friar Gertrid's ghost entered the scene.

Seeing it, William Wallace said, "Ha! If thou are what thou appear to be, step forward. Speak! I have faced more horrid terror."

"Where dost gang?" Friar Gertrid's ghost said.

[Where do thou go?]

"What's that to thee?" William Wallace asked.

Friar Gertrid's ghost said:

"Thou'll not lestand lang;

"Two wolves will suck thy bluide; by the third night,

"I charge thy soul will meet mine. Thy death is dight."

[Thou will not last long;

[Two wolves will suck thy blood; by the third night,

[I state that thy soul will meet mine. Thy death is ordained.]

"Thou are a lying spirit," William Wallace said.

Friar Gertrid's ghost said:

"Bruce byn thy bane;

"Gif on thou gang, look not turn back again.

"Wallace, beware! Methinks it thee should irk,

"Mare need hast thou to serve God in the kirk."

[Bruce is thy bane;
[If thou go on, don't look to turn back again.
[Wallace, beware! I think this should irk thee,
[For thou have more need to serve God in the church.]
William Wallace said:
"Stay! If thou have a voice, then thou are blood and bone as I am.
"Let me feel thee, or else I'll think thee are a sorcerous imaginary sound.
"Withstand me! Stand here for me.
"Thou are some English damned witch that from a reverend friar has stolen his shape to abuse me."
William Wallace continued:
"Stop! Are thou going?"
Friar Gertrid's ghost exited, beckoning for William Wallace to follow.
William Wallace said:
"No, hag, I will not!
"It spoke surely: With confidence it told me Bruce should be my bane —"
Old Wallace's ghost entered the scene.
Seeing it, William Wallace said:
"That eye has shot me through — it wounds me to death.
"I know that face too well, but it is so ghastly that I'd rather with my fingernails here dig my grave than once more behold thee.
"Part from me, vexed spirit; my blood turns to water."
As Old Wallace's ghost exited, William Wallace said:
"I beseech thee, don't frighten me — it's gone!"
Peggy's ghost entered the scene.
Peggy's ghost said:
"Alack, Scotland, to whom salt thou complain!
"Alack, fra' mourning, wha sall thee refrain?
"I thee beseekand for Him [Who] died on tree,
"Come not near Bruce, yet Bruce sall not hurt thee.
"Alack! Alack! No man can stand 'gainst fate.
"The damp dew fra the heaven does 'gin to fall;
"I to my rest mim gang ere the cock craw."
[Woe, Scotland, to whom shall thou complain!
[Woe, when shall thee refrain from mourning?

[I beseech thee for Him Who died on the cross,

[Go not near Bruce, yet Bruce shall not hurt thee.

[Woe! Woe! No man can stand against fate.

[The damp dew from the heaven does begin to fall;

[I must go to my rest before the cock crows.]

Peggy's ghost exited.

William Wallace said:

"It was my wife! What horror do I meet here?

"No armor in the world can hold out fear."

Grimsby, a still-living man, entered the scene.

He said, "We wait for your instructions."

"Whom did you meet on your way here?" William Wallace asked.

"Nobody," Grimsby said.

"Did you see nothing?" William Wallace asked.

"I didn't see anything," Grimsby answered.

William Wallace said:

"It was my brain's weakness, then.

"I have seen strange sights, which soon I'll tell.

"If, Grimsby, we meet never anymore, farewell."

William Wallace exited.

Alone, Grimsby said to himself:

"Huh, I am struck dumb. Oh, man's slippery fate!

"Mischiefs that follow us at our backs, we shun,

"And are struck down with those we dream not on."

He exited.

— 5.3. —

Menteith and Comyn talked together in Glasgow Moor.

"I have also held private conversation with Vallance, Sheriff of Fife. He, in Edward Longshanks' name, swears to me we shall have good preferment, besides the promised gold," Menteith said.

"Preferment" meant good things, such as titles.

"Peace!" Comyn said. "Silence! Wallace comes!"

"Has Robert the Bruce come?" Menteith asked.

"It is not yet his hour to come," William Wallace answered.

"Who came along with you?" Menteith asked.

"My footboy — my page — only," William Wallace answered. "He is tying up my horse."

Menteith said quietly to himself, "I must kill that page."

He said out loud to William Wallace, "I'll look and see whether Bruce is in sight yet."

"Do," William Wallace said.

Monteith exited.

"You are sad," Comyn said.

"My mind is shaken, but the storm is over," William Wallace replied.

A cry sounded: "Help! Murder!"

"What cry is that?" William Wallace asked.

Menteith returned and said, "Be armed! Bruce, with a force, comes to betray thee. From some villain's hand, thy footboy has been murdered."

"Murdered?" William Wallace said. "Bruce shall repent this deed!"

"So shall thou," Menteith said.

"Away with him!" Comyn said.

Some soldiers entered, knocked William Wallace down, and then they hurried him away while he was unconscious.

Everyone exited.

119

— 5.4 —

Suspecting treachery, Robert Bruce, his face hidden by his cloak, said to a soldier loyal to him, "Help to disguise me, soldier. In exchange, take these clothes for thine, and here's some gold to boot."

"To boot" means "in addition."

They exchanged clothing, and Robert Bruce gave the soldier some gold.

"Even if I am hanged in all my splendid clothing, my Lord, I don't care," the soldier said.

"Shh!" Robert Bruce whispered. "I ask thee to seal up thy lips and eyes. Neither see nor tell anyone where I am."

"I won't, my Lord," the soldier said.

"Oh, my poor wronged country!" Robert Bruce said. "Pardon me, heaven, and with a feather plucked from mercy's wing brush off the purple spots that otherwise would grow like freckles on my soul."

Mercy can be personified as a winged angel.

The purple spots were his sins against Scotland; they were likened to the red rash of secondary syphilis.

Percy and Clifford entered the scene.

"My Lord, here comes company," the soldier said to Robert Bruce.

"Here, quick!" Robert Bruce said. "Give me my own clothing again and get thee gone!"

Again, they exchanged clothes.

"Sirrah, soldier, did thou see the Earl of Huntingdon?" Percy asked.

Robert Bruce was the Earl of Huntingdon. Percy and Clifford did not see him.

"Huntingdon?" the soldier asked.

"The Lord Bruce, I mean," Clifford said.

"Who calls for Bruce?" Robert Bruce said.

Percy said to Clifford, "His face is hidden by his cloak, and he is alone. I'll go to the king."

"Do, sirrah," Clifford said. "Be gone!"

Percy exited.

"To where has Percy gone?" Robert Bruce said. "He asked for Bruce."

"There's great enquiry for you," Clifford said.

"By whom?" Robert Bruce asked.

"The king has a fresh command for Bruce," Clifford answered.

"For me?" Robert Bruce said. "He may command his subjects."

"True, and Huntingdon is one," Clifford said.

He meant Robert Bruce, the Earl of Huntingdon.

"Is none," Robert Bruce said.

"No subject?" Clifford asked.

Robert Bruce said:

"None who dare oppose your king."

He then said to himself:

"Oh, my impostumed — infected — spleen will fly into their faces."

This society regarded the spleen as the source of anger and ill will.

Robert Bruce then said out loud:

"What command has England now?"

"England" meant the King of England: King Edward I.

"Fresh powers are to be levied which Bruce of Huntingdon must lead," Clifford answered.

"Against whom?" Robert Bruce asked.

"Against proud Wallace," Clifford answered. "Against the Scots."

"I will not!" Robert Bruce said. "I am not his butcher. I will not fight against the Scots."

"What!" Clifford said. "Will not?

"No," Robert Bruce said. "I will not, Clifford."

"Peace!" Clifford said. "Be silent!"

Robert Bruce said:

"My Lord, I dare not.

"In this last battle I received some wounds that yet bleed inward. I will no more banquet strangers with my native blood."

The wounds that bleed inward were his sins against Scotland.

"Bruce does not speak like a subject," Clifford said.

Robert Bruce said:

"English Edward does not command like a King.

"Thrice-honored Clifford, I'll trust you with my bosom — with my innermost thoughts."

"No, you shall not," Clifford said. "My virgin honor is so chaste it shall not keep company with a disquiet — disturbed — bosom, nor talk with discontents."

Clifford respected the valiant Scots, but he was loyal to King Edward I.

"It shall not," Robert Bruce said. "I will but —"

"Spare me," Clifford said.

"The air has ears no more," Robert Bruce said. "You sent to me — I will, but tell bold Clifford not a word."

Clifford had sent Robert Bruce gifts that were an oracle.

Robert Bruce was going to follow one interpretation of the oracle and be loyal to Scotland.

"My thoughts own as much honor as their lord," Clifford said.

Cries of "Traitor! Traitor!" sounded.

First Menteith, and then from a different direction, King Edward I, Percy, Hertford, and some followers entered the scene.

"A mutiny?" King Edward I asked. "What noise is this?"

"Menteith, a knight of Scotland," Percy said.

"Keep him away from the king," Clifford advised.

"What do thou come for?" King Edward I asked Clifford.

Menteith said:

"Comyn, who is my countryman, and I have brought a jewel to your Highness that, if it were as right as it is known to be counterfeit, it would be worth a kingdom.

"Wearied with war and pitying the deep wounds that fainting Scotland bears upon her breast and knowing that the only sword that gashes her tender sides is gripped in Wallace's hands, I, in my love for peace and for the safety of two great nations, am the man who laid snares to entrap this monster that devours so many thousand lives.

"The rebel's captured."

"Where is he?" King Edward I asked.

Menteith replied:

"I have brought him to your English camp.

"Force would not do it, but policy. We struck the stag to the ground and thought him dead, but heaven put back and repelled the blow on purpose.

"He's now come to life, from an astonishment — a stupor — when we thought he was dead.

"He is alive so that the world may see the public shame of an arch-traitor."

King Edward I said, "Menteith has won fame and honor by this act. Fetch in this devil."

Menteith exited.

"Thou will have England's thanks but Scotland's curse," Clifford said to himself about Menteith. "Thou never have done better, never worse, damned Judas to thy countryman and friend."

William Wallace, Menteith, and Comyn entered the scene.

"Where am I?" William Wallace asked.

"Here, with Bruce," Robert Bruce said.

William Wallace asked:

"Bruce, my sovereign?"

He looked around and said:

"My blood is sold; this is not Glasgow Moor.

"Some villain has betrayed me."

"Speak to your countrymen, Comyn and Menteith," Clifford said.

William Wallace said:

"Comyn and Menteith?

"Something it was that made the modest night look angry on the world. Aye, this was it, and this was it that cleft my father's grave and raised him from his monumental bed of earth to give me gentle warning."

A tomb is a monument.

William Wallace continued:

"This was it that made my star and my destiny, when all the rest looked pale, blush like a fiery meteor."

William Wallace's star had become a falling star: a meteor.

William Wallace continued:

"Can heaven wink at and ignore this act of betrayal?"

"It can, it does, and at far greater mischiefs," Menteith said.

In this society, the word "mischiefs" had a stronger meaning than it has now. It meant "evils."

"This is not of thy acting?" William Wallace asked.

"Yes, it is of mine," Menteith answered.

"Not here?" William Wallace asked.

"Here, or in Hell," Menteith said.

"Why then, go act such deeds of betrayal there," William Wallace said. "Boast of them there."

William Wallace then said out loud an ambiguous sentence.

His sentence may be punctuated like this: "In that black kingdom, say that a 'base rebel' fell by a 'true subject'!"

In this sentence, which uses ironic quotes, the "'base rebel'" is William Wallace, and the "'true subject'" is Menteith.

In other words: William Wallace is not a base rebel because he is justified in fighting against England, and Menteith is not a true subject to Robert Bruce, who ought to be King of the Scots.

Or his sentence may be punctuated like this: "In that black kingdom, say that a base rebel fell by a true subject!"

In this sentence, which does not use ironic quotes, the "base rebel" is Menteith, and the "true subject" is William Wallace.

In other words: William Wallace is a true subject to Robert Bruce, who ought to be King of the Scots, and Menteith is a base rebel to Scotland.

William Wallace killed Menteith with his fist.

King Edward I, who had been looking at Robert Bruce, asked, "What's that?"

"Your Scotch jeweller has been slain," Clifford said.

Menteith had said that he had brought a jewel — William Wallace — to the king.

"By whom?" King Edward I asked.

"By Wallace," Clifford answered.

"Hear me speak, King Edward," William Wallace requested.

"My good liege, hear him," Clifford said.

King Edward I replied:

"Clifford, I have vowed neither to hear nor to see him.

"Drag him away from here.

"My eye shall not be so compassionate to view him lest I pity him.

"Hang, draw, and quarter him!"

The sentence for traitors was death: Draw the traitor on a hurdle to the place of execution. Hang the traitor until he is almost dead, draw his intestines out of his body and burn them, and chop his body into four parts. Also, the traitor was emasculated and castrated and beheaded.

This is the English law that gives the punishment for high treason:

That you be drawn on a hurdle to the place of execution where you shall be hanged by the neck and being alive cut down, your privy members shall be cut off and your bowels taken out and burned before you, your head severed from your body and your body divided into four quarters to be disposed of at the King's pleasure.

The *Oxford English Dictionary* defines "hurdle" in this way: "A kind of frame or sledge on which traitors used to be drawn through the streets to execution."

Earlier, Friar Gertrid had made a prophecy about William Wallace: "Until thy own blood proves to be false, this crag — your neck — shall never lie dead."

William Wallace's "blood" was two of his fellow Scots: Menteith and Comyn.

"First hear me speak!" William Wallace said.

King Edward I said:

"Drag him hence and let that heart, those limbs, which were the motives — the instruments — to rebellious war be torn asunder, cast upon that ground which he, with unkind steel, so often did wound.

"Away with him!"

William Wallace said:

"Farewell to all the world!

"I have met Death too often to fear him now. It grieves me only that I have not freed Scotland, my native soil, from tyranny.

"Bruce, thou have a kingdom. Don't lose it."

"Stop his throat!" King Edward I ordered.

William Wallace said:

"I go to one, too."

The kingdom he was going to was the Kingdom of Heaven.

He continued:

"And, on my grave, when death has there laid me down, let this be my epitaph: 'My own betrayed me.'"

William Wallace, guarded by soldiers, exited.

"Let him have noble trial," Robert Bruce requested.

King Edward I said:

"He shall have the trial of an arch-traitor."

That meant: No trial.

King Edward I continued:

"Percy and Clifford, take Bruce away from here."

"Take me away?" Robert Bruce asked.

King Edward I said:

"Yes, take you away from here, sir.

"From this hour, I swear never to see thee, Earl of Huntingdon.

"Listen, Clifford and Northumberland. Take him away!"

Percy was the Earl of Northumberland.

"What is King Edward's meaning?" Robert Bruce asked.

King Edward I answered:

"Your head shall feel our meaning."

He again ordered Clifford and Northumberland:

"See it dispatched."

Robert Bruce began, "You may —"

Guarded by Percy and Clifford, Robert Bruce was taken away.

"My honored Lord, although untimely death has taken away from here one engine — one instrument — of that work that brought that rebel Wallace to his end, seeing our countries' peace and England's good is, by his death, made perfect and completed, I don't doubt that the promised reward of full ten thousand crowns shall now remain to the survivor," Comyn said.

Menteith was dead, and so Comyn wanted the full ten thousand crowns for himself alone.

"Comyn, I perceive that it was the reward, not love, that was the motive of the deed, but you shall have your due," King Edward I said. "Of that, soon."

Trumpets sounded, and many people entered the scene: Robert Bruce, Percy, Clifford, and others. Bruce was wearing stately clothing for an important occasion.

King Edward I said, "I told thee, Bruce, that thou upon thy head should feel our meaning, and so that all the world may know we value honour above conquest, although we have an army able to turn all Scotland into a chaos, here between both our armies give us thy oath of fealty and wear both the crown and the title of thine ancestors.

"England is full of honor," Robert Bruce said. "Bruce does bow to thy command."

He was then crowned King of the Scots.

King Edward I had said, "From this hour, I swear never to see thee, Earl of Huntingdon."

Now, when he looked at Robert Bruce, he would see Robert Bruce, King of the Scots.

"Give him his oath of fealty," King Edward I said, "and along with him, give the oath of fealty to those lords who are his countrymen."

They swore the oath of fealty.

Robert Bruce then stabbed Comyn.

"Stand back!" Robert Bruce said. "A serpent shall not with his breath infect our kingly ears. Die, slave! For he who would betray his friend shall never serve me."

This society believed that the breath of a serpent was poisonous.

"What has Bruce done?" King Edward I asked.

Robert Bruce answered:

"I have made a sacrifice of honor and revenge; no traitor's hand shall help to lift a crown up to my head."

He said to Comyn:

"Thou did betray, so then die unpitied."

Comyn died.

Clifford said:

"Brave Bruce, I'll love thee for this honored act; thou have performed a noble piece of justice.

"Now shall the Ghost of Old Wallace sleep in peace, and perfect love shall between these lands increase.

"Comyn has his full reward for his foul treason. Drag hence the slave and make him food for crows.

"The lamp that gave rebellion light has spent the oil that fed it; all our spears are turned to palms and olive branches, all our stars are now made whole and our destiny is complete.

"Peace is the balm of wars."

Micah 4.3 states, *And he shall judge among many people, and rebuke strong nations afar off; and they shall beat their swords into plowshares, and their spears into pruninghooks: nation shall not lift up a sword against nation, neither shall they learn war any more* (King James Version).

APPENDIX A: NOTES
— 1.2 —

I'de rather be a Scutchmans whore than an Englishmans waaife, and be dreave toth' Kirke with helters."
(1.2.26-27)
Source of Above:

The Valiant Scot, by J.W.: A Critical Edition. George F. Byers, editor. New York: Garland Pub., 1980. P. 134.

For Your Information:

The tradition, according to the academic encyclopedia "Marriage Customs of the World," dates back to the The Rape of the Sabine Women, an event in Roman mythology where Roman soldiers abducted and raped the women in the surrounding regions. The women were carried off against their will.

Bizarrely, the event turned into a common Roman wedding practice. The bride, according to the encyclopedia, would run off to her mother while the bridegroom and his friends would intercept her and pull her away. And a group of people, not just the groom, would carry the bride into the house.

The most direct interpretation of the tradition is that it's a benign recollection of "marriage by capture." But the encyclopedia also offers a more charitable interpretation: that the wife wants to make a show about how she isn't eager to leave her parents' home and start a family of her own.

Source of Above: Jacob Shamsian, "Here's the horrifying truth about why grooms carry brides across the threshold." *Business Insider.* 31 March 2017 https://www.businessinsider.com/why-carry-bride-across-threshold-meaning-2017-3#:~:text=Grooms%20carry%20brides%20across%20the%20threshold%20of%

— 2.2 —

A few lines appear in George F. Byers's edition that do not appear in Patricia A. Griffin's edition:

My retelling of Patricia A. Griffin's edition:

"Like the pity that thy barbarous son bestowed on my boy's life, I'll print upon thy bosom," Sir Thomas Selby said to Old Wallace.

Sir Thomas Selby stabbed Old Wallace.

Sir William Hazelrigg said, "Thus withered the pride of Lanark, and thus fades the flower that caused their ruin."

He stabbed Peggy and then exited.

Jeffrey Wiseacres said, "Thus religion's cries were stopped with steel, and thus religion dies."

Jeffrey Wiseacres stabbed Friar Gertrid.

Above: Retold from this source:

J. W. Gent. THE VALIANT SCOT. Editor: Patricia A. Griffin. Sheffield Hallam University. 2007. PDF. P. 80.

My retelling of George F. Byers's edition (additional lines not in Ms. Griffin's edition are in italics):

"Like the pity that thy barbarous son bestowed on my boy's life, I'll print upon thy bosom," Sir Thomas Selby said to Old Wallace.

Sir William Hazelrigg said to Peggy, "Like the pity that thy pitiless husband took on the widows' tears and that he took on the cries of the orphans that kissed his knees at Lavercke's massacre, I'll show on thee."

Sir Thomas Selby said to Old Wallace, "Thus fell my son, and thus the father of his murderer falls."

Sir Thomas Selby stabbed Old Wallace.

Sir William Hazelrigg said, "Thus withered the pride of Lanark, and thus fades the flower that caused their ruin."

Sir William stabbed Peggy and then exited.

Jeffrey Wiseacres said, "Thus religion's cries were stopped with steel, and thus religion dies."

Jeffrey Wiseacres stabbed Friar Gertrid.

Above: Retold from this source:

The Valiant Scot, by J.W.: A Critical Edition. George F. Byers, editor. New York: Garland Pub., 1980. Pp. 181-182.

Note: Lavercke's massacre is not described in the play.

— 5.3 —

MENTEITH

Is the Bruyce come?

(5.3.6).

Source of Above:

The Valiant Scot, by J.W.: A Critical Edition. George F. Byers, editor. New York: Garland Pub., 1980. P. 298.

Why is Robert Bruce called Robert the Bruce?

This is his father's name:

Robert de Brus, 6th Lord of Annandale

KING

> *Clifford, I have vow'd 95*
> *Neither to heare nor see him. Drag him hence:*
> *Mine eye shall not be so compassionate*
> *To view him. least I pitie him. Hang,*
> *Draw, and quarter him!*

(5.4.95-99)

Source of Above:

The Valiant Scot, by J.W.: A Critical Edition. George F. Byers, editor. New York: Garland Pub., 1980. P. 308.

For Your Information:

> *Here's the actual text of the English law (on the books until 1870) outlining the death sentence for anyone convicted of high treason:*
>
> *That you be drawn on a hurdle to the place of execution where you shall be hanged by the neck and being alive cut down, your privy members shall be cut off and your bowels taken out and burned before you, your head severed from your body and your body divided into four quarters to be disposed of at the King's pleasure.*

Source of Above: Dave Roos, "The 'Hanged, Drawn and Quartered' Execution Was Even Worse than You Think." HowStuff Works. 29 June 2021

https://history.howstuffworks.com/history-vs-myth/hanging-drawing-and-quartering.htm

The "drawing" part may refer to a different kind of drawing. The traitor was tied to a hurdle, aka sledge, and then drawn — dragged — to the place of execution. And then the traitor was hung, had his intestines drawn out, and was quartered.

The law mentions "privy members." I take that to mean penis and testicles. Emasculation is cutting off the penis. Castration is cutting off the testicles.

APPENDIX B: SHEFFIELD HALLAM UNIVERSITY STUDENT EDITIONS

The Sheffield Hallam University student editions I have looked at are good work and should be made available publicly, perhaps at Kindle Desktop Publishing or draft2create.com.

https://extra.shu.ac.uk/emls/iemls/resources.html

Previously, I used Tim Seccombe's edition of John Ford's *The Queen* when writing my book *John Ford's* The Queen: *A Retelling.*

Text collections

Modern-spelling editions of Cavendish circle plays:

Jane Cavendish and Elizabeth Brackley, *The Concealed Fancies*, ed. Daniel Cadman (2015).

https://extra.shu.ac.uk/emls/iemls/renplays/ConcealedFancies.pdf

Margaret Cavendish, *The Unnatural Tragedy*, ed. Andrew Duxfield (2016).

https://extra.shu.ac.uk/emls/iemls/renplays/
The%20Unnatural%20Tragedy.pdf

"Early Stuart Libels: an edition of poetry from manuscript sources." Ed. Alastair Bellany and Andrew McRae. *Early Modern Literary Studies* Text Series I (2005).

http://purl.oclc.org/emls/texts/libels/

Edited modern-spelling etexts of Renaissance plays, prepared in connection with the *Editing a Renaissance Play* module of Sheffield Hallam University's MA in English Studies:

George Wilkins, *The Miseries of Enforced Marriage*, edited by Rhiannon O'Grady (2002).

https://extra.shu.ac.uk/emls/iemls/renplays/miseries.htm

Thomas May, *The Tragedy of Agrippina*, edited by Lyndsey Clarke (2003).

https://extra.shu.ac.uk/emls/iemls/renplays/mayindex.html

Anonymous, *The Tragedy of Nero*, edited by Tracey Siddle (2004).

https://extra.shu.ac.uk/emls/iemls/renplays/tragedyofnero.htm

Anonymous, *The Tragedy of Claudius Tiberius Nero*, edited by Sharon McDonnell (2004).

https://extra.shu.ac.uk/emls/iemls/renplays/ctneroindex.html

Anonymous, *The Fatal Marriage*, edited by Andrew Duxfield (2004).

https://extra.shu.ac.uk/emls/iemls/renplays/fatalindex.html

Richard Brome, *The City Wit*, edited by Katherine Wilkinson (2004). This text formed the basis for the 2007 production of the play by the Arts Academy, University of Ballarat.

https://extra.shu.ac.uk/emls/iemls/renplays/witindex.htm

Nathaniel Richards, *The Tragedy of Messalina, the Roman Empress*, edited by Samantha Gibbs (2004).

https://extra.shu.ac.uk/emls/iemls/renplays/
mess%20contents%20page.htm

Anonymous, *Lust's Dominion*, edited by Mary Ellen Cacheado (2005). This text was used for the *Lust's Dominion* scenes in a 2008 episode of Channel 4's *Peep Show*.

https://extra.shu.ac.uk/emls/iemls/renplays/lustsdominion.htm

Richard Brome, *The Queen's Exchange*, edited by Richard Wood (2005).

https://extra.shu.ac.uk/emls/iemls/renplays/qexchcontents.htm

Thomas Rawlins, *The Rebellion*, edited by Amy Lockwood (2006).

https://extra.shu.ac.uk/emls/iemls/renplays/rawlreb.htm

Anonymous, *The Valiant Scot*, edited by Pat Griffin (2007).

https://extra.shu.ac.uk/emls/iemls/renplays/valiantscot/contents.htm

Jasper Fisher, *Fuimus Troes*, edited by Chris Butler (2007).

https://extra.shu.ac.uk/emls/iemls/renplays/fuimustroes.htm

John Ford, *The Queen,* edited by Tim Seccombe (2008).

https://extra.shu.ac.uk/emls/iemls/renplays/queencontents.htm

Thomas Heywood, *The Rape of Lucrece*, edited by Chris Bailey (2009).

https://extra.shu.ac.uk/emls/iemls/renplays/rapelucrece/contents.html

Gervase Markham and Lewis Machin, *The Dumb Knight*, edited by Kris Towse (2009).

https://extra.shu.ac.uk/emls/iemls/renplays/dumbknight.htm

Samuel Daniel, *The Tragedy of Cleopatra*, edited by Lucy Knight (2011).

https://extra.shu.ac.uk/emls/iemls/renplays/cleopatra.html

Anon, *A Warning for Fair Women*, edited by Gemma Leggott (2011).

https://www.google.com/
search?client=safari&rls=en&q=renplays%2FA+Warning+for+Fair+Wom

A pdf downloads when you click on the link on the website.

Anon., *Two Lamentable Tragedies*, edited by Gemma Leggott (2011).

https://www.google.com/
search?client=safari&rls=en&q=renplays%2FTwo+Lamentable+Tragedies

A pdf downloads when you click on the link on the website.

Individual etexts

John Spencer Hill. *John Milton: Poet, Priest and Prophet. A Study of Divine Vocation in Milton's Poetry and Prose.*
Romuald I. Lakowski, "A Bibliography of Thomas More's *Utopia.*"
https://extra.shu.ac.uk/emls/01-2/lakomore.html
Romuald I. Lakowski. Sir Thomas More and the Art of Dialogue. Ph.D. Diss. U of British Columbia, Fall 1993.
https://extra.shu.ac.uk/emls/iemls/work/chapters/lakowski.html
R.G. Siemens, "Milton's Works and Life: Select Studies and Resources." *Early Modern Literary Studies*, iEMLS Postprint <URL: http://purl.oclc.org/ emls/iemls/postprint/CCM2Biblio.html>. Originally published in Dennis Danielson (ed.). *The Cambridge Companion to Milton.* 2nd ed. Cambridge, 1999. Pp. 268-90.

APPENDIX C: ABOUT THE AUTHOR

It was a dark and stormy night. Suddenly a cry rang out, and on a hot summer night in 1954, Josephine, wife of Carl Bruce, gave birth to a boy — me. Unfortunately, this young married couple allowed Reuben Saturday, Josephine's brother, to name their first-born. Reuben, aka "The Joker," decided that Bruce was a nice name, so he decided to name me Bruce Bruce. I have gone by my middle name — David — ever since.

Being named Bruce David Bruce hasn't been all bad. Bank tellers remember me very quickly, so I don't often have to show an ID. It can be fun in charades, also. When I was a counselor as a teenager at Camp Echoing Hills in Warsaw, Ohio, a fellow counselor gave the signs for "sounds like" and "two words," then she pointed to a bruise on her leg twice. Bruise Bruise? Oh yeah, Bruce Bruce is the answer!

Uncle Reuben, by the way, gave me a haircut when I was in kindergarten. He cut my hair short and shaved a small bald spot on the back of my head. My mother wouldn't let me go to school until the bald spot grew out again.

Of all my brothers and sisters (six in all), I am the only transplant to Athens, Ohio. I was born in Newark, Ohio, and have lived all around Southeastern Ohio. However, I moved to Athens to go to Ohio University and have never left.

At Ohio U, I never could make up my mind whether to major in English or Philosophy, so I got a bachelor's degree with a double major in both areas, then I added a Master of Arts degree in English and a Master of Arts degree in Philosophy. Yes, I have my MAMA degree.

Currently, and for a long time to come (I eat fruits and veggies), I am spending my retirement writing books such as *Nadia Comaneci: Perfect 10*, *The Funniest People in Comedy*, *Homer's* Iliad: *A Retelling in Prose*, and *William Shakespeare's* Hamlet: *A Retelling in Prose*.

If all goes well, I will publish one or two books a year for the rest of my life. (On the other hand, a good way to make God laugh is to tell Her your plans.)

By the way, my sister Brenda Kennedy writes romances such as *A New Beginning* and *Shattered Dreams*.

APPENDIX D: SOME BOOKS BY DAVID BRUCE

Retellings of a Classic Work of Literature

Arden of Faversham: *A Retelling*

Ben Jonson's The Alchemist: *A Retelling*

Ben Jonson's The Arraignment, or Poetaster: *A Retelling*

Ben Jonson's Bartholomew Fair: *A Retelling*

Ben Jonson's The Case is Altered: *A Retelling*

Ben Jonson's Catiline's Conspiracy: *A Retelling*

Ben Jonson's The Devil is an Ass: *A Retelling*

Ben Jonson's Epicene: *A Retelling*

Ben Jonson's Every Man in His Humor: *A Retelling*

Ben Jonson's Every Man Out of His Humor: *A Retelling*

Ben Jonson's The Fountain of Self-Love, or Cynthia's Revels: *A Retelling*

Ben Jonson's The Magnetic Lady, or Humors Reconciled: *A Retelling*

Ben Jonson's The New Inn, or The Light Heart: *A Retelling*

Ben Jonson's Sejanus' Fall: *A Retelling*

Ben Jonson's The Staple of News: *A Retelling*

Ben Jonson's A Tale of a Tub: *A Retelling*

Ben Jonson's Volpone, or the Fox: *A Retelling*

Christopher Marlowe's Complete Plays: Retellings

Christopher Marlowe's Dido, Queen of Carthage: *A Retelling*

Christopher Marlowe's Doctor Faustus: *Retellings of the 1604 A-Text and of the 1616 B-Text*

Christopher Marlowe's Edward II: *A Retelling*

Christopher Marlowe's The Massacre at Paris: *A Retelling*

Christopher Marlowe's The Rich Jew of Malta: *A Retelling*

Christopher Marlowe's Tamburlaine, Parts 1 and 2: *Retellings*

Dante's Divine Comedy: *A Retelling in Prose*

Dante's Inferno: *A Retelling in Prose*

Dante's Purgatory: *A Retelling in Prose*

Dante's Paradise: *A Retelling in Prose*

The Famous Victories of Henry V: *A Retelling*

From the Iliad *to the* Odyssey: *A Retelling in Prose of Quintus of Smyrna's* Posthomerica

George Chapman, Ben Jonson, and John Marston's Eastward Ho! *A Retelling*

George Peele's The Arraignment of Paris: *A Retelling*

George Peele's The Battle of Alcazar: *A Retelling*

George's Peele's David and Bathsheba, and the Tragedy of Absalom: *A Retelling*

George Peele's Edward I: *A Retelling*

George Peele's The Old Wives' Tale: *A Retelling*

George-a-Greene: *A Retelling*

The History of King Leir: *A Retelling*

Homer's Iliad: *A Retelling in Prose*

Homer's Odyssey: *A Retelling in Prose*

J.W. Gent.'s The Valiant Scot: *A Retelling*

Jason and the Argonauts: A Retelling in Prose of Apollonius of Rhodes' Argonautica

John Ford: Eight Plays Translated into Modern English

John Ford's The Broken Heart: *A Retelling*

John Ford's The Fancies, Chaste and Noble: *A Retelling*

John Ford's The Lady's Trial: *A Retelling*

John Ford's The Lover's Melancholy: *A Retelling*

John Ford's Love's Sacrifice: *A Retelling*

John Ford's Perkin Warbeck: *A Retelling*

John Ford's The Queen: *A Retelling*

John Ford's 'Tis Pity She's a Whore: *A Retelling*

John Lyly's Campaspe: *A Retelling*

John Lyly's Endymion, The Man in the Moon: *A Retelling*

John Lyly's Galatea: *A Retelling*

John Lyly's Love's Metamorphosis: *A Retelling*

John Lyly's Midas: *A Retelling*

John Lyly's Mother Bombie: *A Retelling*

John Lyly's Sappho and Phao: *A Retelling*

John Lyly's The Woman in the Moon: *A Retelling*

John Webster's The White Devil: *A Retelling*

King Edward III: *A Retelling*

Mankind: *A Medieval Morality Play* (A Retelling)

Margaret Cavendish's The Unnatural Tragedy: *A Retelling*

The Merry Devil of Edmonton: *A Retelling*

The Summoning of Everyman: *A Medieval Morality Play* (A Retelling)

Robert Greene's Friar Bacon and Friar Bungay: *A Retelling*

The Taming of a Shrew: *A Retelling*

Tarlton's Jests: A Retelling

Thomas Middleton's A Chaste Maid in Cheapside: *A Retelling*

Thomas Middleton's Women Beware Women: *A Retelling*

Thomas Middleton and Thomas Dekker's The Roaring Girl: *A Retelling*

Thomas Middleton and William Rowley's The Changeling: *A Retelling*

The Trojan War and Its Aftermath: Four Ancient Epic Poems

Virgil's Aeneid: *A Retelling in Prose*

William Shakespeare's 5 Late Romances: Retellings in Prose

William Shakespeare's 10 Histories: Retellings in Prose

William Shakespeare's 11 Tragedies: Retellings in Prose

William Shakespeare's 12 Comedies: Retellings in Prose

William Shakespeare's 38 Plays: Retellings in Prose

William Shakespeare's 1 Henry IV, aka Henry IV, Part 1: A Retelling in Prose

William Shakespeare's 2 Henry IV, aka Henry IV, Part 2: A Retelling in Prose

William Shakespeare's 1 Henry VI, aka Henry VI, Part 1: A Retelling in Prose

William Shakespeare's 2 Henry VI, aka Henry VI, Part 2: A Retelling in Prose

William Shakespeare's 3 Henry VI, aka Henry VI, Part 3: A Retelling in Prose

William Shakespeare's All's Well that Ends Well: A Retelling in Prose

William Shakespeare's Antony and Cleopatra: A Retelling in Prose

William Shakespeare's As You Like It: A Retelling in Prose

William Shakespeare's The Comedy of Errors: A Retelling in Prose

William Shakespeare's Coriolanus: A Retelling in Prose

William Shakespeare's Cymbeline: A Retelling in Prose

William Shakespeare's Hamlet: A Retelling in Prose

William Shakespeare's Henry V: A Retelling in Prose

William Shakespeare's Henry VIII: A Retelling in Prose

William Shakespeare's Julius Caesar: A Retelling in Prose

William Shakespeare's King John: A Retelling in Prose

William Shakespeare's King Lear: A Retelling in Prose

William Shakespeare's Love's Labor's Lost: A Retelling in Prose

William Shakespeare's Macbeth: A Retelling in Prose

William Shakespeare's Measure for Measure: A Retelling in Prose

William Shakespeare's The Merchant of Venice: A Retelling in Prose

William Shakespeare's The Merry Wives of Windsor: A Retelling in Prose

William Shakespeare's A Midsummer Night's Dream: A Retelling in Prose

William Shakespeare's Much Ado About Nothing: A Retelling in Prose

William Shakespeare's Othello: A Retelling in Prose

William Shakespeare's Pericles, Prince of Tyre: A Retelling in Prose

William Shakespeare's Richard II: A Retelling in Prose

William Shakespeare's Richard III: A Retelling in Prose

William Shakespeare's Romeo and Juliet: A Retelling in Prose

William Shakespeare's The Taming of the Shrew: A Retelling in Prose

William Shakespeare's The Tempest: A Retelling in Prose

William Shakespeare's Timon of Athens: A Retelling in Prose

William Shakespeare's Titus Andronicus: A Retelling in Prose

William Shakespeare's Troilus and Cressida: A Retelling in Prose

William Shakespeare's Twelfth Night: A Retelling in Prose

William Shakespeare's The Two Gentlemen of Verona: A Retelling in Prose

William Shakespeare's The Two Noble Kinsmen: A Retelling in Prose

William Shakespeare's The Winter's Tale: A Retelling in Prose